The New York Times

IN THE HEADLINES

Tech Addiction

EDUCATIONAL PUBLISHING BOOKS

THE NEW YORK TIMES EDITORIAL STAFF

Published in 2020 by New York Times Educational Publishing
in association with The Rosen Publishing Group, Inc.
29 East 21st Street, New York, NY 10010

First Edition

The New York Times
Caroline Que: Editorial Director, Book Development
Phyllis Collazo: Photo Rights/Permissions Editor
Heidi Giovine: Administrative Manager

Rosen Publishing
Megan Kellerman: Managing Editor
Xina M. Uhl: Editor
Greg Tucker: Creative Director
Brian Garvey: Art Director

Cataloging-in-Publication Data
Names: New York Times Company.
Title: Tech addiction / edited by the New York Times editorial staff.
Description: New York : The New York Times Educational Publishing, 2020. | Series: In the headlines | Includes glossary and index.
Identifiers: ISBN 9781642823608 (library bound) | ISBN 9781642823592 (pbk.) | ISBN 9781642823615 (ebook)
Subjects: LCSH: Internet addiction. | Information technology—Social aspects. | Information technology—Psychological aspects.
Classification: LCC RC569.5.I54 T434 2020 | DDC 616.85'84—dc23

Manufactured in the United States of America

On the cover: While technology continues to develop at breakneck speed, its results are not always positive. Tech addiction has resulted in mental health issues, overuse injuries, privacy challenges and concern about its long-term effects; Andia/Universal Images Group/Getty Images.

Contents

CHAPTER 2

Handheld Wonderland

CHAPTER 3

Dangers for Young and Old

Introduction

IN TODAY'S WORLD, it is almost impossible to avoid technology entirely. The Internet, smartphones, video games and dating apps have changed the way people work, shop, communicate, entertain themselves, learn and find romantic partners. While easy access to information, communication with people worldwide and innovations in business have had mostly positive effects on everyday living, there are risks of mental health problems, overuse injuries, privacy challenges and the possibility that adults and children alike may suffer long-term effects from obsessive use of tech.

Technology addiction can manifest as addictive behavior in regard to any platform or device. Such behavior has been recognized in relation to online gambling, gaming, Internet pornography, auction sites such as eBay and more. It can result in information overload and persistent disruptions to everyday life.

In 2018, mental health clinician Dr. Shainna Ali reported in a Psychology Today article that excessive use of technology is associated with a number of harmful effects. These include reduced physical fitness and poor posture from the sedentary lifestyle it encourages, visual problems such as eye strain and headaches, injuries from not paying attention while walking or driving, infections from devices with excessive germs, limited social interaction that causes isolation, sleep deprivation and a host of psychological problems including depression, poor confidence and emotional instability.

Troublesome tech use encompasses more than just that of desktop computers at home, work or school, too: smartphones, tablets, laptops and an increasing array of "smart" objects like certain car models and televisions also provide opportunities to overrely on and overuse tech.

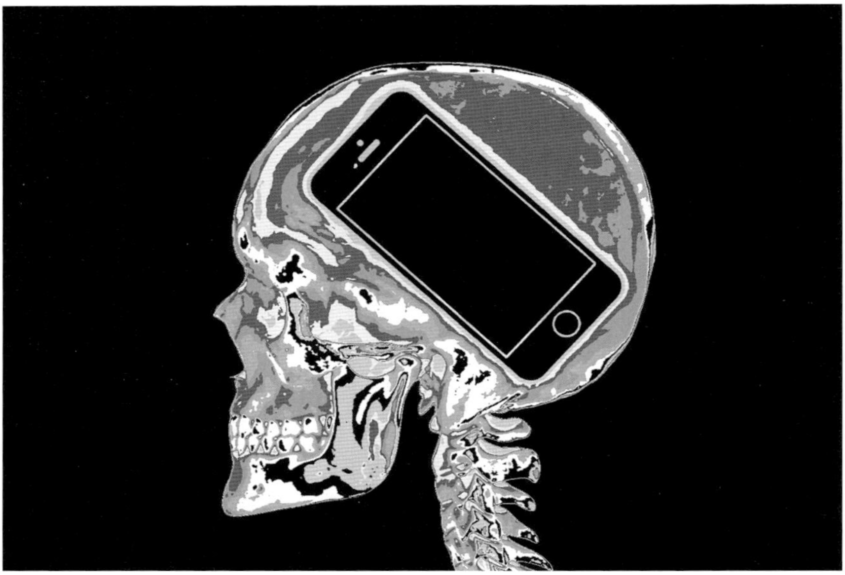

ERIC CARTER

With further advancements and so many devices that are made for use on the go, the risk of spending most of one's time looking at a screen has increased significantly over the last few decades.

The possibilities of Internet access have spawned new generations of games, financial institutions, government services, educational products and business applications. While the utility of such services makes life easier in many ways, there are notable drawbacks to such convenience. For instance, the sheer amount of information and connectivity to work and friends has accelerated daily existence to a frantic pace for many people. The problem affects users both in the United States and abroad, as seen in the articles collected here about China and South Korea.

In a culture that is increasingly tech-heavy and online, other issues can crop up as well. Sexting, or the sending of sexually provocative images over the Internet, is done not only by consenting adults, but by ever younger users of social media apps where the images do not automatically disappear — they may follow someone for their entire lives, unfairly affecting future work prospects and romantic relationships. Children as young as three years old have become Internet celebrities, demonstrating that even for the preschool set, tech is a potent force. While parents are often criticized when they allow their children to use devices too frequently, others downplay the risks and point out the skills that these children are learning may help them later in the job market.

Though appropriate access to different apps and devices is debated depending on the age group or relationship between users, the correlation between some tech-addictive behaviors and real-world consequences is undeniable. Using a mobile device while driving or walking can lead to injuries and even death. Relationships can suffer when parents or spouses isolate themselves and avoid interaction due to obsessive tech use.

Even people at tech giants Facebook and Google have voiced concern over the prevalence of Internet and tech use in daily life. Although so many of the devices and platforms people use are relatively new, they have been assimilated into the mainstream so effectively that it can be easy to forget that the long-term effects are not yet fully understood. Now more than ever, it's important to become aware of the impact of tech addiction in the modern world.

CHAPTER 1

The Internet Comes Alive

In the late 1980s, computers became affordable enough that the general population and businesses began to use them in increasing numbers. As the digital world played a growing role in finance, government and other areas, criminals adapted their techniques to take advantage of people's reliance on technology. Internet pornography grew in popularity. The impact of information overflow began to worry experts as reports of computer addiction started to appear from around the world, prompting some governments to begin tracking web usage.

Computers: An Extra Becomes an Essential

BY DIRK JOHNSON | JUNE 18, 1986

WESTON, CONN., JUNE 17 — The young artist burst into giggles, tickled by her portrait's mischievous grin, or perhaps its green hair.

Kindergarteners still give life to such exotic creatures. But now they draw with computers, as well as with crayons, sometimes changing green hair to blue by pushing a button.

In Weston, and many other suburban school districts, the computer has become as essential to the classroom as the blackboard. Even as students are learning to print, they are becoming familiar with floppy disks and the importance of pressing the "save" button.

"Formal word processing," said Eileen Bengtson, an elementary school teacher in the district, "doesn't start until the first grade."

The expanded computer classes represent perhaps the most striking change in curriculum in suburban schools in a move toward a more rigorous academic regimen.

More than just teaching data processing, computers are reshaping course instruction, from mathematics to music. Beginning this year, for example, the district's industrial arts students are drafting by computer.

And next year, music students will compose melodies for the computer to play. History classes will re-fight the Battle of Antietam through computer simulation. And English students will check spellings by pressing a command on the word processing programs.

"These children might one day be shopping by computer, banking by computer," Mrs. Bengtson said. "This will be a valuable tool for them for the rest of their lives."

This school district of 1,500 students now has more than 120 computers, representing the biggest increase in recent school spending.

COMPUTERS ENHANCE CLASSES

Teachers are now turning to computer programs for supplementary course material in the manner they once used filmstrips. The drill-and-practice programs on computers allow students to forge ahead as soon as they have successfully completed a task, rather than wait for the rest of the class. Conversely, students who need more time for a problem are not unnecessarily rushed.

The correction capabilities of computers, teachers said, help build confidence among students when they know a mistake can be erased by pushing the delete button. "Students feel like they can be more daring," said George Miller, director of computer services at the high school. "It's the end of the white-out correction."

Moreover, high achievers in computer courses are not necessarily those who excel in other subjects. For these students, the new-found talents have brought new meaning and fulfillment to education.

The science of computers, once considered a section within mathematics, has become an educational department in its own right in the school district. All students at the middle-school level must take a course in computer literacy. And by the end of eighth grade, most students here have mastered computer skills sufficient "to get an entry-level job in data processing," said John Marshall, a middle school computer instructor.

MODELED ON COLLEGE COURSES

In the high school, an advanced course has been modeled after first-year computer science courses at the best universities. A 16-year-old student in the advanced course this year designed a spread sheet that plans for retirement investment. "Some of these students are ahead of us," said Mr. Miller, the computer director.

Yet, Mr. Miller said: "We're finding that we don't have that many students interested in the higher levels of science. Instead, we're finding many students who see computers as a way to make life easier. And that's the computer revolution: people who are not necessarily 'into' computers being able to use the technology."

Outside the classroom, the use of computers in the schools has also expanded. Administrative and financial records are kept on computers. And at the guidance office, students can extract information about colleges that would otherwise take them hours of paging through catalogues.

A student simply tells the computer, in effect: "I want a college in the Northeast, with an enrollment of less than 1,500, noted for its courses in paleontology and Chinese history, with tuition costs under $3,500. My college board scores are. ..."

The computer delivers the appropriate list of colleges. If the list is too large, the student can add new criteria to the equation to pare down the possibilities.

'SIGHT, SOUND AND MOTION'

By learning to use computers earlier, teachers said, the students do not develop the fears about the technology that are common among adults, including some teachers. Many of the students have used computers at home, teachers said, even before they entered kindergarten.

"Like riding a bike, it's easier to learn when you're younger," Mrs. Bengtson said. "The children are very turned on by the medium. There's sight, sound and motion. And there's immediate feedback."

The younger students learn to use computers much like playing a game. The computer program for kindergarteners features the Wise Owl who points to the correct letter to be pushed. A character named Zebug flutters in the air and cheers when the task is completed appropriately.

When a little girl inserted her disk and typed in her name, the computer responded: "Hi Greer! Let's draw a picture." In many ways, the picture exercise resembles the Etch A Sketch toy.

'YOU MEAN IT'S GONE?'

In another program, an animated character challenges the student to pick the correct answer before the allotted time expires. "If you are late," the character warns, "I will crash." Meanwhile, a freckled boy sat before a blank computer screen and raised his arms in despair. He had forgotten to push the save button. "You mean it's gone?" the boy asked. It happens to the best, a teacher's aide assured him.

Even the youngest students are instructed in the ethics of computer use. Teachers talk, for example, about computer "hackers," those who illegally break into corporate or government security systems, or invade the privacy of other computer users.

"It's a terrific tool," Mrs. Bengtson said she tells the students, "but it can be misused."

As a form of recreation, computers are transforming after-school activities. The students with computers at home frequently belong to data centers that give them access to others around the country with whom they can socialize on a technological level, sending messages over telephone lines.

Some students have formed new friendships through these “bulletin boards” and more than a few have tallied up frightening telephone bills through the avocation.

“It’s the 1980’s version of pen pals,” said Mr. Miller, the high school instructor.

When Machines Spawn Obsession

BY PETER H. LEWIS | NOV. 13, 1988

Is there such a thing as computer addiction? Experts say yes, although its dangers remain unclear.

THE PHENOMENON IS familiar in the world of "hackers": a young man of exceptional intelligence, feeling that he is alienated from the system and threatened by the real world, finds safety in the computer lab and develops an obsession for the technology. Shunning sleep, and limiting social relationships to the sphere of hackers with whom he shares his obsession, he pushes himself to his physical and mental limits in the quest for the ultimate hack, the fusion of elegant thought and computer code.

Such might be the profile of the person responsible for the recent successful computer virus attack on a national military network. But some psychologists say that a variation on the phenomenon is also emerging in corporate culture. A crippling obsession with computer technology is affecting business executives as well as hackers.

Male executives and managers — the victims are almost always men, for reasons that are not fully understood — are often found working late into the night at the office or at home, silhouetted in their solitude by the eerie green light of the computer screen. The effects of this obsession can be found in a person's personal as well as professional life.

For companies, this could be a problem in the making, even though few managers object to employees who work overtime on productive tasks. In fact, these obsessed computer workers can be some of the most valuable employees at a company.

And these workers differ from "hackers" in their productivity: Unlike hackers, who use computers for thrills and personal satisfaction, the obsessed workers use their machines as tools to perform a task or in some other goal-oriented way. Indeed, companies — both big and small — often benefit from a worker's obsession with the computer, even if it is at the expense of the individual's personal life.

But in the long run the obsession can detract from an employee's effectiveness on the job. The worker may "burn out" as a result of endless hours at the computer. Stress, muscular and skeletal problems, fatigue and eyestrain, among other health problems, have been associated with extended computer use.

Business and personal relationships suffer because the man cannot pull himself away from the keyboard. The rationale is often "just one more" — one more printout, one more recalculation, one more revision. One task leads to the next and the perception of time becomes distorted, particularly as the user becomes oblivious to the passage of time. When the user finally breaks away, his thoughts are preoccupied with the next session at the keyboard.

Is this computer addiction? Can computers become as destructively addictive to susceptible executives as alcohol, drugs, cigarettes, sex or work itself?

"I have no doubt at all that it occurs," said Jack Dunham, a professor who specializes in psychology and microtechnology at the University of Texas, who has been an observer of computer culture since 1960. "Just look around."

Michael Dertouzos, director of the laboratory of computer science at the Massachusetts Institute of Technology, said that while there is definitely a phenomenon of computer addiction — "I have observed it in myself and in thousands of my students over the past 25 years," he said — whether it is harmful or not is open to debate.

"I am a hacker," he said. "I have a Mac II. I helped design the thing, and I'm at it constantly. My family complains, but they get used to it. And it's a lot of fun. Some men golf, some play baseball."

Marvin Minsky, an artificial intelligence researcher at M.I.T., has long defended the hacker as no different from others who are seriously devoted to their work.

But other — more personal — issues surface in discussions of men who are obsessed with their computers. Power and control are words that inevitably turn up, and the ramifications of their link with computer use can be seen at home and on the job.

"The tendency to sit in front of the machine forever was incredible," said Dr. Dertouzos. "It's a power trip, a sense of tremendous control over a machine that does not behave as unpredictably as some of our friends." He added: "The very things that men seem to treasure — power and control — are there."

Perhaps, Dr. Dunham suggested, there is such a person as a "puterfiliac," who feels that he lacks control in the corporate culture and finds control, power and a higher sense of self-esteem in working on a computer that does his bidding, loyally, patiently and predictably.

Dr. Dunham surmised that computer addiction, like other forms of addiction, is based on psychological denial, "a substitute or escape mechanism from some reality that they don't want to face."

"It's a safe place for someone to get away," he said. "It's demanding enough that it gets you into it. And yet it's easy to rationalize because hey, it's my job, I have to do it."

A societal element is there, too, he said. "It's also socially acceptable, just like smoking, gambling or alcohol used to be acceptable addictions."

In discussing computer addiction, the experts consider it almost exclusively a male problem. Why are men, more so than women, so prone to it?

David Zubrow, a planning research analyst at Carnegie Mellon University in Pittsburgh, who is studying the issue of gender and technology, said studies have confirmed what has been obvious for years. "Males compute more than women," he said. "A higher proportion of males get involved in computing. Males like computers more than women do."

But, he asked, "is sex an explanation?" The answer is unclear. Mr. Zubrow said he was looking for other explanations. But so far they, too, are not illuminating. "What processes produce what we observe as gender differences?" he asked. "They may have little to do with computing."

The Lure of Data: Is It Addictive?

BY MATT RICHTEL | JULY 6, 2003

THIS IS CHARLES Lax's brain on speed.

Mr. Lax, a 44-year-old venture capitalist, is sitting in a conference for telecommunications executives at a hotel near Los Angeles, but he is not all here. Out of one ear, he listens to a live presentation about cable television technology; simultaneously, he surfs the Net on a laptop with a wireless connection, while occasionally checking his mobile device — part phone, part pager and part Internet gadget — for e-mail.

Mr. Lax flew from Boston and paid $2,000 to attend the conference, called Vortex. But he cannot unwire himself long enough to give the presenters his complete focus. If he did, he would face a fate worse than lack of productivity: he would become bored.

"It's hard to concentrate on one thing," he said, adding: "I think I have a condition."

The ubiquity of technology in the lives of executives, other businesspeople and consumers has created a subculture of the Always On — and a brewing tension between productivity and freneticism. For all the efficiency gains that it seemingly provides, the constant stream of data can interrupt not just dinner and family time, but also meetings and creative time, and it can prove very tough to turn off.

Some people who are persistently wired say it is not uncommon for them to be sitting in a meeting and using a handheld device to exchange instant messages surreptitiously — with someone in the same meeting. Others may be sitting at a desk and engaging in conversation on two phones, one at each ear. At social events, or in the grandstand at their children's soccer games, they read news feeds on mobile devices instead of chatting with actual human beings.

These speed demons say they will fall behind if they disconnect, but they also acknowledge feeling something much more powerful:

they are compulsively drawn to the constant stimulation provided by incoming data. Call it O.C.D. — online compulsive disorder.

"It's magnetic," said Edward M. Hallowell, a psychiatry instructor at Harvard. "It's like a tar baby: the more you touch it, the more you have to."

Dr. Hallowell and John Ratey, an associate professor at Harvard and a psychiatrist with an expertise in attention deficit disorder, are among a growing number of physicians and sociologists who are assessing how technology affects attention span, creativity and focus. Though many people regard multitasking as a social annoyance, these two and others are asking whether it is counterproductive, and even addicting.

The pair have their own term for this condition: pseudo-attention deficit disorder. Its sufferers do not have actual A.D.D., but, influenced by technology and the pace of modern life, have developed shorter attention spans. They become frustrated with long-term projects, thrive on the stress of constant fixes of information, and physically crave the bursts of stimulation from checking e-mail or voice mail or answering the phone.

"It's like a dopamine squirt to be connected," said Dr. Ratey, who compares the sensations created by constantly being wired to those of narcotics — a hit of pleasure, stimulation and escape. "It takes the same pathway as our drugs of abuse and pleasure."

"It's an addiction," he said, adding that some people cannot deal with down time or quiet moments. "Without it, we are in withdrawal."

According to research compiled by David E. Meyer, a psychology professor at the University of Michigan, multitaskers actually hinder their productivity by trying to accomplish two things at once. Mr. Meyer has found that people who switch back and forth between two tasks, like exchanging e-mail and writing a report, may spend 50 percent more time on those tasks than if they work on them separately, completing one before starting the other.

As a result, Mr. Meyer said, businesspeople who multitask "are making themselves worse businesspeople."

He says little research has been done into why some people are compulsively drawn to multitasking. But he theorizes that the allure has several layers. Multitasking offers a guise of productivity, a "macho" show of accomplishment, and similarities to a quick amphetamine rush.

"It's related to what happens to skydivers or jet pilots," he said. "They put themselves in situations where, if they don't perform at peak efficiency, they'll crash and burn. In the aftermath there is a rush of chemicals."

Patrick P. Gelsinger, the chief technology officer at Intel, says it is clear that the overall time spent in front of screens — whether desktop computers or handheld devices — is rising. "Time spent watching television is down," he said. "But over all you see a discretionary increase in the amount of time people are connected to technology."

The presence of such devices, as well as their power, will only grow. Networks that provide wireless Internet access are in their early stages. Intel has put the full force of its science and marketing effort behind wireless devices and the superfast miniature microprocessors that power them.

Intel portrays computers as pushing productivity, and Mr. Gelsinger scoffs at the idea that digital devices have a compulsive or physically addictive draw. "We don't make drugs," he said. "We make technology building blocks that move the world forward in all ways."

But he concedes that there can be a point at which the constant accessibility of information is hard to escape.

In one meeting at Intel, Mr. Gelsinger said he found himself sending an instant message to his boss across the room — a potential distraction, though he argued that by doing so, he did not have to engage in "disruptive whispering." At other times, Mr. Gelsinger has had to remind himself not to use e-mail on his laptop during a meeting because it can send the message that he is not paying full attention.

Sometimes, discipline must be imposed from the outside. At a recent technology conference organized by The Wall Street Journal and attended by industry heavyweights like Bill Gates of Microsoft, Steve Jobs of Apple Computer and Stephen M. Case of AOL Time Warner, people were discouraged from using their wireless Internet access during presentations.

Bucking the recent tradition at trade shows and technology conferences, the organizers decided not to provide wireless Internet access inside the conference.

"We wanted people to absorb what the speakers were saying," said Walt Mossberg, a technology columnist at The Journal.

"We decided that if you have Wi-Fi, it would be destructive," he added. "If you have the Internet, it will win out. People imagine they can multitask, but sometimes people overestimate the extent to which they can do it."

If multitasking creates a problem for people, the cause is not the gadget makers themselves, said Jeff Hallock, the senior director for consumer products at Sprint PCS, the mobile telephone carrier. The company has been selling the manna of multitasking: phones that can also take digital pictures, send e-mail and instant messages and download music. But Mr. Hallock says those functions help people stay organized, not make them frenetic.

"We're enhancing people's lives so they can have more control of the flurry of activity that's seemingly coming in," he said.

"You don't have to check your voice mail," he added. "We're giving you the chance to do so."

The notion that using all these devices creates a harmful addiction is absurd to Bruce P. Mehlman, assistant commerce secretary for technology policy and a former executive at Cisco Systems. Mr. Mehlman said the presence of many gadgets in people's lives created not a cacophony, but harmony and balance.

Mobile phones, wireless Internet devices and laptops have liberated executives, he said, allowing them to leave the office and to spend more time at home. The users of these technologies are constantly wired, he said, but to a very positive goal.

"Ten years ago, you had to be in the office 12 hours," said Mr. Mehlman, who said he now spent 10 hours a day at work, giving him more time with his wife and three children, while also making use of his wireless-enabled laptop, BlackBerry and mobile phone.

"I get to help my kids get dressed, feed them breakfast, give them a bath and read them stories at night," he said. He can also have Lego air fights — a game in which he and his 5-year-old son have imaginary dogfights with Lego airplanes.

Both love the game, and it has an added benefit for Dad: he can play with one hand while using the other to talk on the phone or check e-mail. The multitasking maneuver occasionally requires a trick: although Mr. Mehlman usually lets his son win the Lego air battles, he sometimes allows himself to win, which forces his son to spend a few minutes putting his plane back together.

"While he rebuilds his plane, I check my e-mail on the BlackBerry," Mr. Mehlman explained.

Mr. Lax, too, cannot pass up the chance to use every bit of technology that comes his way. A graduate of Boston University who lives outside Boston, he is managing general partner at GrandBanks Capital, a venture investment firm. He serves on the boards of three companies, working to turn them into successful ventures. "I build companies one customer at a time," he said, adding that his investments are up against other well-financed competitors. "It's a race against time."

Mr. Lax uses technology to keep up. He is, by his own admission, "Always On."

On his office desk is a land-line telephone, a mobile phone, a laptop computer connected to several printers, and a television, often tuned to CNN or CNBC. At his side is the aptly named Sidekick, a mobile device that serves as camera, calendar, address book, instant-messaging gadget and fallback phone. It can browse the Internet and receive e-mail. He has been known to pick it up whenever it chirps at him — and he acknowledges having used it to check e-mail while in the men's restroom.

There is no down time in the car, either. "I talk on the phone, but I have a headset," Mr. Lax said. Does he do anything else, like using his Sidekick to read e-mail? "I won't be quoted as saying what else I do because it could get me arrested," he said, laughing.

Mr. Lax said he loved the constant stimulation. "It's instant gratification," he said, and it staves off boredom. "I use it when I'm in a waiting situation — if I'm standing in line, waiting to be served for lunch, or getting takeout coffee at Starbucks. And, my God, at the airport it's disastrous to have to wait there.

"Being able to send an e-mail in real time is just — " Mr. Lax paused. "Can you hold for a second? My other line is ringing."

When he returned, he said he shared this way of working with many venture capitalists. "We all suffer a kind of A.D.D," he said. "It's a bit of a joke, but it's true. We are easily bored. We have lots of things going on at the same time."

The technology gives him a way to direct his excess energy. "It is a kind of Ritalin," he said, referring to the drug commonly taken by people with attention deficit disorder.

But he said technology dependence could have its down side. "I'm in meetings all the time with people who are focused on what they're doing on their computers, not on the presentation," he said.

During the Vortex telecommunications conference, held in May in Dana Point, Calif., he and dozens of others were using wireless Internet access. He said that he was paying attention to the speaker, using his Internet connection to look up information about the cable industry.

"I was supporting the effort of the speaker by figuring the elements he was talking about," Mr. Lax said. He paused. "I was also doing e-mail so I guess I wasn't giving 100 percent," he added. "I was 40 percent supporting the effort, and 60 percent doing other things."

Indeed, he said, the technology can be a bit distracting. "But it's not a problem," he said. "Being able to process lots of data allows me to be more efficient and productive."

"It allows me to accelerate success."

Hooked on the Web: Help Is on the Way

BY SARAH KERSHAW | DEC. 1, 2005

REDMOND, WASH. — The waiting room for Hilarie Cash's practice has the look and feel of many a therapist's office, with soothing classical music, paintings of gentle swans and colorful flowers and on the bookshelves stacks of brochures on how to get help.

But along with her patients, Dr. Cash, who runs Internet/Computer Addiction Services here in the city that is home to Microsoft, is a pioneer in a growing niche in mental health care and addiction recovery.

The patients, including Mike, 34, are what Dr. Cash and other mental health professionals call onlineaholics. They even have a diagnosis: Internet addiction disorder.

These specialists estimate that 6 percent to 10 percent of the approximately 189 million Internet users in this country have a dependency that can be as destructive as alcoholism and drug addiction, and they are rushing to treat it. Yet some in the field remain skeptical that heavy use of the Internet qualifies as a legitimate addiction, and one academic expert called it a fad illness.

Skeptics argue that even obsessive Internet use does not exact the same toll on health or family life as conventionally recognized addictions. But, mental health professionals who support the diagnosis of Internet addiction say, a majority of obsessive users are online to further addictions to gambling or pornography or have become much more dependent on those vices because of their prevalence on the Internet.

But other users have a broader dependency and spend hours online each day, surfing the Web, trading stocks, instant messaging or blogging, and a fast-rising number are becoming addicted to Internet video games.

Dr. Cash and other professionals say that people who abuse the Internet are typically struggling with other problems, like depression and anxiety. But, they say, the Internet's omnipresent offer of escape from reality, affordability, accessibility and opportunity for anonymity can also lure otherwise healthy people into an addiction.

Dr. Cash's patient Mike, who was granted anonymity to protect his privacy, was at high risk for an Internet addiction, having battled alcohol and drug abuse and depression. On a list of 15 symptoms of Internet addiction used for diagnosis by Internet/Computer Addiction Services, Mike, who is unemployed and living with his mother, checked off 13, including intense cravings for the computer, lying about how much time he spends online, withdrawing from hobbies and social interactions, back pain and weight gain.

A growing number of therapists and inpatient rehabilitation centers are often treating Web addicts with the same approaches, including 12-step programs, used to treat chemical addictions.

Because the condition is not recognized in psychiatry as a disorder, insurance companies do not reimburse for treatment. So patients either pay out of pocket, or therapists and treatment centers bill for other afflictions, including the nonspecific impulse control disorder.

There is at least one inpatient program, at Proctor Hospital in Peoria, Ill., which admits patients to recover from obsessive computer use. Experts there said they see similar signs of withdrawal in those patients as in alcoholics or drug addicts, including profuse sweating, severe anxiety and paranoid symptoms.

And the prevalence of other technologies — like BlackBerry wireless e-mail devices, sometimes called CrackBerries because they are considered so addictive; the Treo cellphone-organizer; and text messaging — has created a more generalized technology addiction, said Rick Zehr, the vice president of addiction and behavioral services at Proctor Hospital.

The hospital's treatment program places all its clients together for group therapy and other recovery work, whether the addiction is to cocaine or the computer, Mr. Zehr said.

"I can't imagine it's going to go away," he said of technology and Internet addiction. "I can only imagine it's going to continue to become more and more prevalent."

There are family therapy programs for Internet addicts, and interventionists who specialize in confronting computer addicts.

Among the programs offered by the Center for Online Addiction in Bradford, Pa., founded in 1994 by Dr. Kimberly S. Young, a leading researcher in Internet addiction, are cyberwidow support groups for the spouses of those having online affairs, treatment for addiction to eBay and intense behavioral counseling — in person, by telephone and online — to help clients get Web sober.

Another leading expert in the field is Dr. Maressa Hecht Orzack, the director of the Computer Addiction Study Center at McLean Hospital in Belmont, Mass., and an assistant professor at Harvard Medical School. She opened a clinic for Internet addicts at the hospital in 1996, when, she said, "everybody thought I was crazy."

Dr. Orzack said she got the idea after she discovered she had become addicted to computer solitaire, procrastinating and losing sleep and time with her family.

When she started the clinic, she saw two patients a week at most. Now she sees dozens and receives five or six calls daily from those seeking treatment elsewhere in the country. More and more of those calls, she said, are coming from people concerned about family members addicted to Internet video games like EverQuest, Doom 3 and World of Warcraft.

Still, there is little hard science available on Internet addiction.

"I think using the Internet in certain ways can be quite absorbing, but I don't know that it's any different from an addiction to playing the violin and bowling," said Sara Kiesler, professor of computer science and human-computer interaction at Carnegie Mellon University. "There is absolutely no evidence that spending time online, exchanging e-mail with family and friends, is the least bit harmful. We know that people who are depressed or anxious are likely to go online for escape and that doing so helps them."

It was Professor Kiesler who called Internet addiction a fad illness. In her view, she said, television addiction is worse. She added that she was completing a study of heavy Internet users, which showed the majority had sharply reduced their time on the computer over the course of a year, indicating that even problematic use was self-corrective.

She said calling it an addiction "demeans really serious illnesses, which are things like addiction to gambling, where you steal your family's money to pay for your gambling debts, drug addictions, cigarette addictions." She added, "These are physiological addictions."

But Dr. Cash, who began treating Internet addicts 10 years ago, said that Internet addiction was a potentially serious illness. She said she had treated suicidal patients who had lost jobs and whose marriages had been destroyed because of their addictions.

She said she was seeing more patients like Mike, who acknowledges struggling with an addiction to online pornography but who also said he was obsessed with logging on to the Internet for other reasons. He said that he became obsessed with using the Internet during the 2000 presidential election and that now he feels anxious if he does not check several Web sites, mostly news and sports sites, daily.

"I'm still wrestling with the idea that it's a problem because I like it so much," Mike said.

Three hours straight on the Internet, he said, is a minor dose. The Internet seemed to satisfy "whatever urge crosses my head."

Several counselors and other experts said time spent on the computer was not important in diagnosing an addiction to the Internet. The question, they say, is whether Internet use is causing serious problems, including the loss of a job, marital difficulties, depression, isolation and anxiety, and still the user cannot stop.

"The line is drawn with Internet addiction," said Mr. Zehr of Proctor Hospital, "when I'm no longer controlling my Internet use. It's controlling me." Dr. Cash and other therapists say they are seeing a growing number of teenagers and young adults as patients, who grew up spending hours on the computer, playing games and sending instant messages. These patients appear to have significant developmental problems, including attention deficit disorder and a lack of social skills.

A report released during the summer by the Pew Internet and American Life Project found that teenagers did spend an increasing amount of time online: 51 percent of teenage Internet users are online daily, up from 42 percent in 2000. But the report did not find a withering of social skills. Most teenagers "maintain robust networks of friends," it noted.

Some therapists and Internet addiction treatment centers offer online counseling, including at least one 12-step program for video game addicts, which is controversial. Critics say that although it may be a way to catch the attention of someone who needs face-to-face treatment, it is akin to treating an alcoholic in a brewery, mostly because Internet addicts need to break the cycle of living in cyberspace.

A crucial difference between treating alcoholics and drug addicts, however, is that total abstinence is usually recommended for recovery from substance abuse, whereas moderate and manageable use is the goal for behavioral addictions.

Sierra Tucson in Arizona, a psychiatric hospital and behavioral health center, which treats substance and behavioral addictions, has begun admitting a rising number of Internet addicts, said Gina Ewing, its intake manager. Ms. Ewing said that when such a client left treatment, the center's counselors helped plan ways to reduce time on the computer or asked those who did not need to use the Web for work to step away from the computer entirely.

Ms. Ewing said the Tucson center encouraged its Internet-addicted clients when they left treatment to attend open meetings of Alcoholics Anonymous or Narcotics Anonymous, which are not restricted to alcoholics and drug addicts, and simply to listen. Or perhaps, if they find others struggling with the same problem, and if those at the meeting are amenable, they might be able to participate.

"It's breaking new ground," Ms. Ewing said. "But an addiction is an addiction."

DANGER SIGNS FOR TOO MUCH OF A GOOD THING

Fifteen signs of an addiction to using the Internet and computers, according to Internet/Computer Addiction Services in Redmond, Wash., follow:

1. Inability to predict the amount of time spent on computer.

2. Failed attempts to control personal use for an extended period of time.

3. Having a sense of euphoria while on the computer.

4. Craving more computer time.

5. Neglecting family and friends.

6. Feeling restless, irritable and discontent when not on the computer.

7. Lying to employers and family about computer activity.

8. Problems with school or job performance as a result of time spent on the computer.

9. Feelings of guilt, shame, anxiety or depression as a result of time spent on the computer.

10. Changes in sleep patterns.

11. Health problems like carpal tunnel syndrome, eye strain, weight changes, backaches and chronic sleep deprivation.

12. Denying, rationalizing and minimizing adverse consequences stemming from computer use.

13. Withdrawal from real-life hobbies and social interactions.

14. Obsessing about sexual acting out through the use of the Internet.

15. Creation of enhanced personae to find cyberlove or cybersex.

In Korea, a Boot Camp Cure for Web Obsession

BY MARTIN FACKLER | NOV. 18, 2007

MOKCHEON, SOUTH KOREA — The compound — part boot camp, part rehab center — resembles programs around the world for troubled youths. Drill instructors drive young men through military-style obstacle courses, counselors lead group sessions, and there are even therapeutic workshops on pottery and drumming.

But these young people are not battling alcohol or drugs. Rather, they have severe cases of what many in this country believe is a new and potentially deadly addiction: cyberspace.

They come here, to the Jump Up Internet Rescue School, the first camp of its kind in South Korea and possibly the world, to be cured.

South Korea boasts of being the most wired nation on earth. In fact, perhaps no other country has so fully embraced the Internet. Ninety percent of homes connect to cheap, high-speed broadband, online gaming is a professional sport, and social life for the young revolves around the "PC bang," dim Internet parlors that sit on practically every street corner.

But such ready access to the Web has come at a price as legions of obsessed users find that they cannot tear themselves away from their computer screens.

Compulsive Internet use has been identified as a mental health issue in other countries, including the United States. However, it may be a particularly acute problem in South Korea because of the country's nearly universal Internet access.

It has become a national issue here in recent years, as users started dropping dead from exhaustion after playing online games for days on end. A growing number of students have skipped school to stay online, shockingly self-destructive behavior in this intensely competitive society.

Up to 30 percent of South Koreans under 18, or about 2.4 million

SEOKYONG LEE FOR THE NEW YORK TIMES

Students spend their time exercising and doing group activities to wean them from the Internet.

people, are at risk of Internet addiction, said Ahn Dong-hyun, a child psychiatrist at Hanyang University in Seoul who just completed a three-year government-financed survey of the problem.

They spend at least two hours a day online, usually playing games or chatting. Of those, up to a quarter million probably show signs of actual addiction, like an inability to stop themselves from using computers, rising levels of tolerance that drive them to seek ever longer sessions online, and withdrawal symptoms like anger and craving when prevented from logging on.

To address the problem, the government has built a network of 140 Internet-addiction counseling centers, in addition to treatment programs at almost 100 hospitals and, most recently, the Internet Rescue camp, which started this summer. Researchers have developed a checklist for diagnosing the addiction and determining its severity, the K-Scale. (The K is for Korea.)

In September, South Korea held the first international symposium on Internet addiction.

"Korea has been most aggressive in embracing the Internet," said Koh Young-sam, head of the government-run Internet Addiction Counseling Center. "Now we have to lead in dealing with its consequences."

Though some health experts here and abroad question whether overuse of the Internet or computers in general is an addiction in the strict medical sense, many agree that obsessive computer use has become a growing problem in many countries.

Doctors in China and Taiwan have begun reporting similar disorders in their youth. In the United States, Dr. Jerald J. Block, a psychiatrist at Oregon Health and Science University, estimates that up to nine million Americans may be at risk for the disorder, which he calls pathological computer use. Only a handful of clinics in the United States specialize in treating it, he said.

"Korea is on the leading edge," Dr. Block said. "They are ahead in defining and researching the problem, and recognize as a society that they have a major issue."

The rescue camp, in a forested area about an hour south of Seoul, was created to treat the most severe cases. This year, the camp held its first two 12-day sessions, with 16 to 18 male participants each time. (South Korean researchers say an overwhelming majority of compulsive computer users are male.)

The camp is entirely paid for by the government, making it tuition-free. While it is too early to know whether the camp can wean youths from the Internet, it has been receiving four to five applications for each spot. To meet demand, camp administrators say they will double the number of sessions next year.

During a session, participants live at the camp, where they are denied computer use and allowed only one hour of cellphone calls a day, to prevent them from playing online games via the phone. They also follow a rigorous regimen of physical exercise and group activities,

SEOKYONG LEE FOR THE NEW YORK TIMES

Lee Chang-hoon, 15, runs an obstacle course at the Jump Up Internet Rescue School. He spent almost all of his time online before his mother sent him to the camp. "Seventeen hours a day online is fine," he said at the camp.

like horseback riding, aimed at building emotional connections to the real world and weakening those with the virtual one.

"It is most important to provide them experience of a lifestyle without the Internet," said Lee Yun-hee, a counselor. "Young Koreans don't know what this is like."

Initially, the camp had problems with participants sneaking away to go online, even during a 10-minute break before lunch, Ms. Lee said. Now, the campers are under constant surveillance, including while asleep, and are kept busy with chores, like washing their clothes and cleaning their rooms.

One participant, Lee Chang-hoon, 15, began using the computer to pass the time while his parents were working and he was home alone. He said he quickly came to prefer the virtual world, where he seemed to enjoy more success and popularity than in the real one.

He spent 17 hours a day online, mostly looking at Japanese comics and playing a combat role-playing game called Sudden Attack. He played all night, and skipped school two or three times a week to catch up on sleep.

When his parents told him he had to go to school, he reacted violently. Desperate, his mother, Kim Soon-yeol, sent him to the camp.

"He didn't seem to be able to control himself," said Mrs. Kim, a hairdresser. "He used to be so passionate about his favorite subjects" at school. "Now, he gives up easily and gets even more absorbed in his games."

Her son was reluctant at first to give up his pastime.

"I don't have a problem," Chang-hoon said in an interview three days after starting the camp. "Seventeen hours a day online is fine." But later that day, he seemed to start changing his mind, if only slightly.

As a drill instructor barked orders, Chang-hoon and 17 other boys marched through a cold autumn rain to the obstacle course. Wet and shivering, Chang-hoon began climbing the first obstacle, a telephone pole with small metal rungs. At the top, he slowly stood up, legs

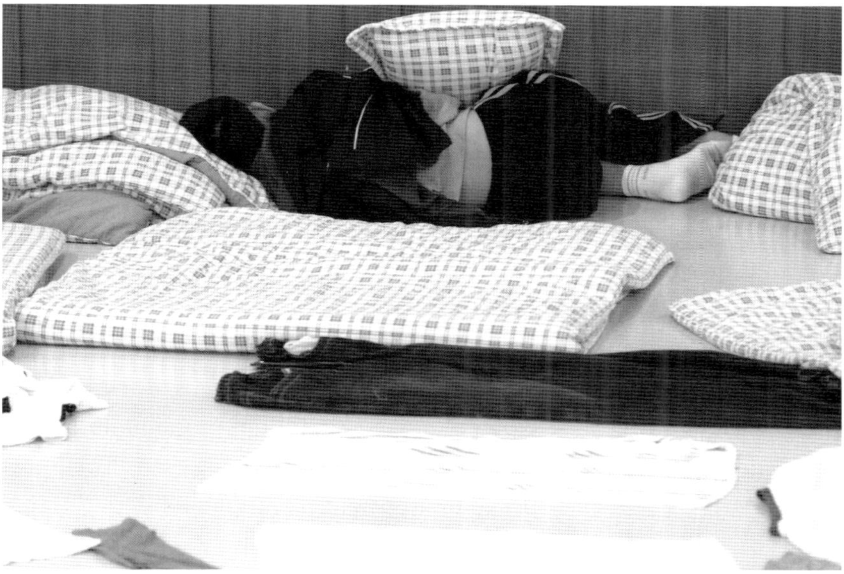

SEOKYONG LEE FOR THE NEW YORK TIMES

Campers are under constant surveillance, even while they sleep.

quaking, arms outstretched for balance. Below, the other boys held a safety rope attached to a harness on his chest.

"Do you have anything to tell your mother?" the drill instructor shouted from below.

"No!" he yelled back.

"Tell your mother you love her!" ordered the instructor.

"I love you, my parents!" he replied.

"Then jump!" ordered the instructor. Chang-hoon squatted and leapt to a nearby trapeze, catching it in his hands.

"Fighting!" yelled the other boys, using the English word that in South Korea means the rough equivalent of "Don't give up!"

After Chang-hoon descended, he said, "That was better than games!"

Was it thrilling enough to wean him from the Internet?

"I'm not thinking about games now, so maybe this will help," he replied. "From now on, maybe I'll just spend five hours a day online."

The Government and the Web

EDITORIAL | BY THE NEW YORK TIMES | AUG. 24, 2009

THE OBAMA ADMINISTRATION is considering new rules to make it easier for government Web sites to use "cookies" and other technology to track visitors. There are valid reasons for using such tools, but the government has to build in robust privacy protections.

The Clinton administration adopted a rule severely limiting tracking on federal Web sites. Tracking could be done only if officials could prove a compelling need and the agency head had personally authorized it.

Tracking technology can help improve the quality of Web sites by monitoring how many people are visiting and how they use the site, and by personalizing the experience. For example, the Parks Service could offer information based on where a user lives.

Browser makers have made it easier for users to remove cookies or even reject them wholesale. But tracking technology can still present a real privacy risk, especially for the uninitiated. If users give personal information on one government Web site, the government could track visits to its other Web sites, like one offering information on drug addiction or H.I.V./AIDS. It could do this with cookies, or by keeping track of users' IP addresses, which may be tied to specific individuals.

In recent years, the government has monitored some Americans' library use and illegally eavesdropped on telephone calls and e-mail. Privacy groups are concerned that the new rules could pave the way for third parties to collect large amounts of data through government sites — for example, if an agency site posted a YouTube video carrying its own cookies.

The Office of Management and Budget is developing the new rules. Officials say they recognize that people must be told that their use of Web sites is being tracked — and be given a chance to opt out. More is needed. The government should commit to displaying such notices prominently on all Web pages — and to making it easy for users to choose not to be tracked.

It must promise that tracking data will be used only for the purpose it was collected for: if someone orders a pamphlet on living with cancer, it should not end up in a general database. Information should be purged regularly and as quickly as possible. These rules must apply to third parties that operate on government sites.

The Obama administration is working to better harness the power of the Internet to deliver government services. That is good. But it needs to be mindful that people should be able to get help and be assured that their privacy is being vigilantly protected.

Feel Like a Wallflower? Maybe It's Your Facebook Wall

BY JENNA WORTHAM | APRIL 9, 2011

ONE RECENT RAINY NIGHT, I curled up on my couch with popcorn and Netflix Instant, ready to spend a quiet night at home. The peace was sweet — while it lasted. Soon, my iPhone began flashing with notifications from a handful of social networking sites, each a beacon of information about what my friends were doing.

As the alerts came in, my mind began to race. Three friends, I learned, had arrived at a music venue near my apartment. But why? What was happening there? Then I saw pictures of other friends enjoying fancy milkshakes at a trendy restaurant. Suddenly, my simple domestic pleasures paled in comparison with the things I could be doing.

The flurry of possibilities set off a rush of restlessness and indecision. I was torn between nesting in my cozy roost or rallying for an impromptu rendezvous, and I just didn't know what to do.

My problem is emblematic of the digital era. It's known as FOMO, or "fear of missing out," and refers to the blend of anxiety, inadequacy and irritation that can flare up while skimming social media like Facebook, Twitter, Foursquare and Instagram. Billions of Twitter messages, status updates and photographs provide thrilling glimpses of the daily lives and activities of friends, "frenemies," co-workers and peers.

The upside is immeasurable. Viewing postings from my friends scattered around the country often makes me feel more connected to them, not less. News and photographs of the bike rides, concerts, dinner parties and nights on the town enjoyed by people in my New York social circle are invaluable as an informal to-do list of local recommendation.

But, occasionally, there is a darker side.

When we scroll through pictures and status updates, the worry that tugs at the corners of our minds is set off by the fear of regret, according to Dan Ariely, author of "Predictably Irrational" and a professor of psychology and behavioral economics at Duke University. He says we become afraid that we've made the wrong decision about how to spend our time.

Streaming social media have an immediacy that is very different from, say, a conversation over lunch recounting the events of the previous weekend. When you see that your friends are sharing a bottle of wine without you — and at that very moment — "you can imagine how things could be different," Professor Ariely said.

It's like a near miss in real life. "When would you be more upset?" he asked. "After missing your flight by two minutes or two hours?

"Two minutes, of course," he said. "You can imagine how things could have been different, and that really motivates us to behave in strange ways."

Fear of missing out does not apply only to those with a hyperactive nightlife.

A friend who works in advertising told me that she felt fine about her life — until she opened Facebook. "Then I'm thinking, 'I am 28, with three roommates, and oh, it looks like you have a precious baby and a mortgage,' " she said. "And then I wanna die."

On those occasions, she said, her knee-jerk reaction is often to post an account of a cool thing she has done, or to upload a particularly fun picture from her weekend. This may make her feel better — but it can generate FOMO in another unsuspecting person.

Caterina Fake, co-founder of Flickr, the photo-sharing service, and of Hunch, a recommendation engine, said, "Social software is both the creator and the cure of FOMO," adding, "It's cyclical."

Some creators of social apps say they have constructed their services to make people keep coming back for more, but not for any insidious purpose.

"No one likes to perform in a vacuum," said Kevin Systrom, the chief executive of Instagram, a mobile photo-sharing application, which allows users to make comments about pictures. The more creative or striking a photograph, the more likely it is to attract favorable attention.

The feedback, Mr. Systrom said, can be slightly addictive. People using Instagram “are rewarded when someone likes it and you keep coming back,” he said.

Whatever angst people may feel when they see someone else having a good time, he said, is probably exaggerated by the overall effect of so many new social data streams pouring into browsers and mobile phones at once.

“We aren’t used to seeing the world as it happens,” he said. “We as humans can only process so much data.”

Of course, fear of missing out is hardly new. It has been induced throughout history by such triggers as newspaper society pages, party pictures and annual holiday letters — and e-mail — depicting people at their festive best. But now, Ms. Fake said, instead of receiving occasional polite updates, we get reminders around the clock, mainlined via the device of our choosing.

Sherry Turkle, a professor at the Massachusetts Institute of Technology and author of “Alone Together,” says that as technology becomes ever more pervasive, our relationship to it becomes more intimate, granting it the power to influence decisions, moods and emotions.

“In a way, there’s an immaturity to our relationship with technology,” she said. “It’s still evolving.”

We are struggling with the always-on feeling of connection that the Internet can provide, she said, and we still need to figure out how to limit its influence on our lives. I asked Professor Turkle what people could do to deal with this stress-inducing quandary. She said she would tell herself to “get a grip and separate myself from my iPhone.”

Easier said than done. I’ve tried, but turning off my phone is nearly impossible — I’m not yet ready for that step.

That evening, though, I flipped the phone over to hide its screen. That helped me ignore what my friends were doing. I settled back to enjoy the evening, deciding not to venture out into the cold and misty night.

Miss G.: A Case of Internet Addiction

OPINION | BY VIRGINIA HEFFERNAN | APRIL 9, 2011

THERE ARE CERTAIN popular diversions — television, video games, the Internet — that we pursue so deliriously we end up hating ourselves for loving them. Others we brightly recast as the duties of citizenship: newspapers, public radio, sports.

All the while, cottage industries crop up to freak us out about our every last cultural pursuit. In recent years, it's Internet use that's been styled as potentially sick, and "Internet addiction" a new reason for self-hatred.

If you're inclined to worry about your habits, you may have already stumbled onto a strange and influential self-evaluation questionnaire by Dr. Kimberly Young, a professor of business at St. Bonaventure University. Though Dr. Young developed the test in 1998, early in Web life, it still dominates the Google returns for "Internet addiction" and steadily stirs up anxiety.

Dr. Young told me she believes the Internet is addictive in part because it "allows us to create new personalities and use them to fulfill unmet psychological needs" — which sounds worrying except that art, entertainment and communications systems are designed explicitly to permit self-exploration and satisfy psychological needs.

The way the test loads the cultural dice in favor of reality over fantasy should make hearts sink. In the hierarchy of the test, any real-world task or interaction, no matter how mundane or tedious, is more important — and, worse, ought to be more fulfilling — than online fantasy, research or social life. "Do you neglect household chores to use the Internet?" one question asks, and undone laundry is later cited as a warning sign. "How often do you block out disturbing thoughts about your life with soothing thoughts of the Internet?" goes another question.

Can this really be science? (And might another psychologist find something to admire in a person who quiets his mind with mere thoughts of the Internet?) I wondered whether other habits of cultural consumption were considered pathological enough to inspire tests. The Web carries a few tests for television addiction, and none for movies. Over on operaddiction.com, there are no tests, only recordings to order.

In general, if a pastime is not classy, those who love it are "addicted." Opera and poetry buffs are "passionate."

Virtually all non-work activities have, at one time or another, been represented as craven and diseased. Opera obsession leads to delinquency in Jean-Jacques Beineix's 1981 film "Diva"; an intense movie habit deepens the alienation of the hero of Walker Percy's 1961 novel "The Moviegoer."

Novels themselves, now the signature pursuit of the sound and literate mind, have also been considered toxic, as in the 1797 analysis, "Novel Reading, a Cause of Female Depravity." The 18th-century worry about female literacy is not unlike the contemporary anxiety that Web use above all makes girls vulnerable to "predators": "Without this poison instilled, as it were, into the blood, females in ordinary life would never have been so much the slaves of vice." Taken together, these warnings against the very stuff that makes life worth living often seem either like veiled boasts ("I'm addicted to the symphony!") or just absurd.

So why are authors and educators hellbent on using this shopworn rhetoric when it comes to Internet use?

Two weeks ago, I met a professed Internet addict, a 20-year-old college student in New York named Gabriela. (Like many addicts, she preferred that only her first name be used.) One of Gabriela's professors had told me she slept with her laptop, and was wired in the extreme. She told me she had taken Dr. Young's test and was worried about her Internet habits.

In e-mail, Gabriela struck a note between irony and concern as she described her symptoms. She told me she keeps an extremely late bedtime, sometimes 4 a.m., because she's up noodling around online.

She then described a typical surfing session: "I'll be on Facebook and see a status update of song lyrics, and I'll Google them and find the band name, that I will subsequently Wikipedia and discover that the lead singer is interesting and briefly look at his Twitter and try his music on Grooveshark" — a music search engine and streaming service — "while looking at pictures of him on Tumblr" — the multimedia microblogging platform — "that will lead me to a meme I've never heard of that I'll explore until I find hilarious photos I will subsequently share with friends of mine on Facebook." Gabriela, who sometimes dresses in the futuristic Victoriana known as steampunk, also loves Webcomics, a site for graphic novels and comic books, and Neopets, a game that lets players care for virtual pets.

She indeed sleeps with her laptop in her bed, "partly so I can have my iTunes play my Sleep playlist." Even on the Sabbath, when she refrains from Internet use for religious reasons, she talks and thinks about the Internet. She told me she considers surfing the Web not so much a regimen but "a state of being" that, like a meditative state, took her years to achieve.

Aha. I'm no addiction expert, but Gabriela strikes me as a bright, self-effacing, religious young woman who keeps student hours and prefers logic games, jokes, graphic novels, trivia quizzes, music, Victoriana and socializing on Facebook to prefab pop bands.

This kind of Internet use isn't usefully described as an addiction, even if there's some shirking of chores and insomnia to it. Fantasy life and real life should, ideally, be brought into balance — but no student who's making decent grades needs to get off the Internet just because it would look more respectable or comprehensible to be playing chess, throwing a Frisbee or reading a George Orwell paperback. The Internet as Gabriela uses it simply is intellectual life, and play. She's just the person I'd want for a student, in fact — or a friend, or a daughter.

It's no accident that "search" is the dominant metaphor of the Internet. And it's no accident that the Internet attracts a certain kind of young, dreamy mind at some liberty to find itself — the type that in earlier eras might have been drawn to novels or movies. As Binx Bolling puts it in "The Moviegoer": "What is the nature of the search? you ask. Really it is very simple; at least for a fellow like me. So simple that it is often overlooked. The search is what anyone would undertake if he were not sunk in the everydayness of his own life."

VIRGINIA HEFFERNAN began writing for The Times in 2003 — first as a television critic in the Arts section, then as an Internet columnist at the Sunday Magazine.

A Hacker Tells All

REVIEW | BY J. D. BIERSDORFER | AUG. 12, 2011

CONSIDERING THE FACT that Windows 95 hadn't even been released when federal agents finally caught up with the computer hacker Kevin Mitnick, one might assume his new memoir would be full of stale old tech and techniques that no one in 2011 could possibly care about. But as Mitnick makes clear here, don't jump to conclusions.

While he excelled at infiltrating computer systems from a keyboard and had a sharp memory for numbers, "Ghost in the Wires" (written with William L. Simon) really showcases another of Mitnick's skills: social engineering, or what he describes as "the casual or calculated manipulation of people to influence them to do things they would not ordinarily do." By doing his research and impersonating authority figures over the phone or by e-mail, Mitnick found he could persuade just about anybody — programmers, technicians, even the nice lady at the Social Security Administration — to give him the things he wanted, like passwords, computer chips and personal information about F.B.I. informants on his tail. "People, as I had learned at a very young age, are just too trusting," he writes.

It's this element to his story that makes "Ghost in the Wires" read like a contemporary über-geeky thriller. Many of today's computer viruses and identity-theft scams — and even the recent phone-hacking scandals of certain newspapers — depend on social engineering mixed with a misuse of technology to dupe the unsuspecting. In that regard, Mitnick's memoir also serves as a wake-up call for anyone trying to keep personal information private. (Out of prison since 2000, Mitnick now works as a security consultant.)

Kevin Mitnick grew up as an only child of divorced parents, moving frequently in the Los Angeles area. He was something of a loner, and his early pursuits included studying magic tricks and ham radio. When he was 12, the revelation that he could ride the local bus system free with a $15 punch and books of half-used blank transfer tickets fished out of a Dumpster behind the bus depot gave him a sense of what he could do (legal or otherwise) if he put his mind to it. Even if one is unfamiliar with Mitnick's life story, it's kind of obvious where he's heading here, and it's far beyond the bus routes around San Bernardino County.

In high school, Mitnick developed an obsession with the inner workings of the telephone company's switches and circuits, a hobby known as "phone phreaking" (and one that was shared by the future Apple founders, Steve Jobs and Steve Wozniak, in their own formative years).

By the time he was 17, in 1981, Mitnick was happily spending his time on things like persuading a Pacific Telephone employee to give him Lucille Ball's home number and burrowing into different corporate computer systems. It was also at the age of 17 that he had his first run-in with the authorities for his activities. Thus began a nearly 20-year cat-and-mouse game with law enforcement that makes up much of the book.

Driven by curiosity and compulsion ("There's always something that's more challenging and fun to hack"), Mitnick spent most of his young adulthood pilfering proprietary code from technology companies like Sun Microsystems and Novell, partly so he could look for bugs and security holes to use to his advantage, and partly for the thrill of the hunt. He also spent plenty of time making free calls on his hacked cellphone and going to the gym. As the authorities began to close in on him in 1992, he created several false identities, and went on the run until he was finally nailed in February 1995.

When not recounting his clever exploits, Mitnick devotes chunks of the book to defiantly rebutting myths that became attached to him — for example, that he had hacked into government computer systems. (He does, however, admit to eavesdropping on the National Security Agency's telephone calls.)

With its caper 'n' chase pacing, "Ghost in the Wires" is fairly entertaining, although the prose can veer into pulpy melodrama: "I had to move *now.* I had to get a new identity *now.* I had to get the hell out of my apartment *now!*"

Like many memoirists, Mitnick clearly relishes the chance to have his say all these years later. He mocks some of the more incredible accusations leveled at him by the authorities: that he had repeatedly turned off the phone service of the actress Kristy McNichol, and that he could "whistle into a telephone and launch a nuclear missile from Norad." (Mitnick surmises that the federal prosecutor who made the latter claim probably mixed him up with Matthew Broderick's youthful computer enthusiast in the 1983 cold-war thriller "WarGames.")

Mitnick's sense of humor is evident as he recounts his adventures. When his ingenious combination of a radio scanner and software alerted him to F.B.I. agents' cellphones in the area, he cheekily had a box of doughnuts waiting for them when they raided his apartment.

For those interested in computer history, "Ghost in the Wires" is a nostalgia trip to the quaint old days before hacking (and hackers) turned so malicious and financially motivated. Unlike computer criminals today, Mitnick ignored the credit card numbers he stumbled across in his pursuit of code. He writes: "Anyone who loves to play chess knows that it's enough to defeat your opponent. You don't have to loot his kingdom or seize his assets to make it worthwhile." He summed up his personal motive to the former Wall Street trader Ivan Boesky when they were both in prison: "I didn't do it for the money; I did it for the entertainment."

GHOST IN THE WIRES
My Adventures as the World's Most Wanted Hacker
By Kevin Mitnick with William L. Simon
Illustrated. 413 pp. Little, Brown & Company. $25.99.

J. D. BIERSDORFER is the production editor of the Book Review and writes the Q&A computer column for The Times.

Electroshock Therapy for Internet Addicts? China Vows to End It

BY MIKE IVES | JAN. 13, 2017

HONG KONG — At the Addiction Treatment Center in eastern China, more than 6,000 internet addicts — most of them teenagers — not only had their web access taken away, they were also treated with electroshock therapy.

The center, in Shandong Province, made headlines in September after one of its patients killed her mother in retribution for abuse she had purportedly suffered at the camp during a forced detox regimen.

Now China is trying to regulate camps like the one in Shandong, which have become a last resort for parents exasperated by their child's habit of playing online games for hours on end.

The government has drafted a law that would crack down on the camps' worst excesses, including electroshock and other "physical punishments." Medical specialists welcomed the law, announced this week in China's state-controlled news media, as an initial step toward curbing scandals in the industry.

"It's a very important move for protecting young children," said Tao Ran, the director of the Internet Addiction Clinic at Beijing Military General Hospital.

Dr. Tao said that many Chinese parents believe that the effects of electroshock therapy are fleeting. But he had seen several Chinese teenagers return from boot camps that treat internet addiction showing signs of lasting psychological trauma, he said.

"They didn't talk, were afraid to meet people and refused to leave their homes," he said, referring to his meetings with the teenagers. "They were panicked even to hear the word 'hospital' and 'doctor.' "

Qu Xinjiu, a law professor at China University of Political Science and Law in Beijing, said the belief that parents have supreme jurisdiction over their children, and that even police officers have no right to intervene in family affairs, is widespread in China.

"That's why there are so many parents sending their kids for electroshock therapy, even when outsiders think it's wrong to do so," Professor Qu said.

Figures on the number or growth of internet detox camps in China are scarce, but the camps' methods have been generating concern for years.

The legislation would also limit how much time each day that minors could play online games at home or in internet bars. Providers of the games would be obliged to take measures to monitor and restrict use, such as requiring players to register under their real names.

The law does not yet specify the number of hours allowed, but minors would be prohibited from playing online games anywhere between midnight and 8 a.m.

Dr. Tao said he doubted that the draft law, which was introduced by the State Council, China's cabinet, could be enforced evenly nationwide. Provisions to limit the number of hours spent online probably could be easily flouted, he said.

Many users of Sina Weibo, China's version of Twitter, were even more critical, saying policing teenagers' behavior online seemed impractical and ill-informed.

"I'm afraid it's just empty talk," a Sina Weibo user wrote.

"What about young kids who always go online on their cellphones?" another wrote. "Isn't that also an addiction?"

Game providers and internet bars that did not enforce the law would be subject to fines and possible closure by the government.

Reports in the Chinese news media this week said that lawmakers would accept public comments on the draft law through early February but gave no indication of when it might be put into practice.

In 2009, the Chinese Health Ministry issued guidelines against using electroshock therapy for internet addicts. Trent M. Bax, the author of "Youth and Internet Addiction in China," said that he wondered whether a ban would be any more effective.

Despite the Health Ministry's policy, "punitive practices continue to victimize China's youth" in internet detox camps, said Dr. Bax, an assistant professor of sociology at Ewha Womans University in Seoul, South Korea.

Researchers from Chinese, Taiwanese and German universities wrote in the journal Asia-Pacific Psychiatry in 2014 that the highest prevalence of "problematic internet use" worldwide had been observed in Asia. Christian Montag, the study's lead author, said in an email on Thursday that South Korea had the world's highest rate of problematic internet use, in part because of its large technology sector and online game market. South Korea also offers camps for internet addiction.

Recent scientific evidence indicates that the best treatments for digital addiction appear to be cognitive behavioral therapy in individual and group settings, which often include patients' parents and significant others, said Daria J. Kuss, a specialist on internet and game addiction at Nottingham Trent University in Britain.

Dr. Kuss said that medication can also be effective, especially if internet addiction is accompanied by anxiety or mood disorders, such as depression. But beatings and electroshock therapy "are not commonly used in the treatment of internet and gaming addiction and are to be considered unethical and inhumane," she said.

Officials and psychologists around the world have debated how to measure and regulate extreme internet use. A crucial question, analysts say, is whether to classify the problem as a psychological disorder or as a symptom of underlying disorders.

In a sign of how fluid the debate is in China, the Health Ministry said in 2009 that it would no longer use the term "addiction" to describe how the internet harmed people who used it improperly or excessively.

But a study the same year by the China Youth Association for Network Development, which is led by a committee under the ruling Communist Party, found that more than 24 million Chinese, age 13 to 29, who used the internet were digital addicts.

KAROLINE KAN contributed research from Beijing.

Why We Can't Look Away From Our Screens

BY CLAUDIA DREIFUS | MARCH 6, 2017

IN A NEW BOOK, "Irresistible: The Rise of Addictive Technology and the Business of Keeping Us Hooked," the social psychologist Adam Alter warns that many of us — youngsters, teenagers, adults — are addicted to modern digital products. Not figuratively, but literally addicted.

Dr. Alter, 36, is an associate professor at the Stern School of Business at New York University who researches psychology and marketing. We spoke for two hours last week at the offices of The New York Times. Our conversation has been edited and condensed for clarity and brevity.

Q. *What makes you think that people have become addicted to digital devices and social media?*

A. In the past, we thought of addiction as mostly related to chemical substances: heroin, cocaine, nicotine. Today, we have this phenomenon of behavioral addictions where, one tech industry leader told me, people are spending nearly three hours a day tethered to their cellphones. Where teenage boys sometimes spend weeks alone in their rooms playing video games. Where Snapchat will boast that its youthful users open their app more than 18 times a day.

Behavioral addictions are really widespread now. A 2011 study suggested that 41 percent of us have at least one. That number is sure to have risen with the adoption of newer more addictive social networking platforms, tablets and smartphones.

Q. *How do you define "addiction"?*

A. The definition I go with is that it has to be something you enjoy doing in the short term, that undermines your well-being in the long term — but that you do compulsively anyway.

KARSTEN MORAN FOR THE NEW YORK TIMES

Adam Alter warns that many of us — youngsters, teenagers, adults — are addicted to modern digital products.

We're biologically prone to getting hooked on these sorts of experiences. If you put someone in front of a slot machine, their brain will look qualitatively the same as when they take heroin. If you're someone who compulsively plays video games — not everyone, but people who are addicted to a particular game — the minute you load up your computer, your brain will look like that of a substance abuser.

We are engineered in such a way that as long as an experience hits the right buttons, our brains will release the neurotransmitter dopamine. We'll get a flood of dopamine that makes us feel wonderful in the short term, though in the long term you build a tolerance and want more.

Q. *Do the designers of the new technologies understand what they're doing?*

A. The people who create video games wouldn't say they are looking to create addicts. They just want you to spend as much time as possible with their products.

Some of the games on smartphones require you to give money as you play, so they want to keep you playing. The designers will build into a game a certain amount of feedback, in the same way that slot machines offer an occasional win to hold your interest.

Not surprisingly, game producers will often pretest different versions of a release to see which one is hardest to resist and which will keep your attention longest. It works.

For the book, I spoke with a young man who sat in front of his computer playing a video game for 45 consecutive days! The compulsive playing had destroyed the rest of his life. He ended up at a rehabilitation clinic in Washington State, reSTART, where they specialize in treating young people with gaming dependencies.

Q. *Do we need legislation to protect ourselves?*

A. It's not a bad idea to consider it, at least for online games.

In South Korea and China, there are proposals for something they call Cinderella laws. The idea is to protect children from playing certain games after midnight.

Gaming and internet addiction is a really serious problem throughout East Asia. In China, there are millions of youngsters with it, and they actually have camps where parents commit their children for months and where therapists treat them with a detox regime.

Q. *Why do you claim that many of the new electronic gadgets have fueled behavioral addictions?*

A. Well, look at what people are doing. In one survey, 60 percent of the adults said they keep their cellphones next to them when they sleep. In another survey, half the respondents claimed they check their emails during the night.

Moreover, these new gadgets turn out to be the perfect delivery devices for addictive media. If games and social media were once confined to our home computers, portable devices permit us to engage with them everywhere.

Today, we're checking our social media constantly, which disrupts work and everyday life. We've become obsessed with how many "likes" our Instagram photos are getting instead of where we are walking and whom we are talking to.

Q. *Where's the harm in this?*

A. If you're on the phone for three hours daily, that's time you're not spending on face-to-face interactions with people. Smartphones give everything you need to enjoy the moment you're in, but they don't require much initiative.

You never have to remember anything because everything is right in front of you. You don't have to develop the ability to memorize or to come up with new ideas.

I find it interesting that the late Steve Jobs said in a 2010 interview that his own children didn't use iPads. In fact, there are a surprising number of Silicon Valley titans who refuse to let their kids near certain devices. There's a private school in the Bay Area and it doesn't allow any tech — no iPhones or iPads. The really interesting thing about this school is that 75 percent of the parents are tech executives.

Learning about the school pushed me to write, "Irresistible." What was it about these products that made them, in the eyes of experts, so potentially dangerous?

Q. *You have an 11-month-old son. How do you interact with your technologies when you're with him?*

A. I try not to use my phone around him. It's actually one of the best mechanisms to force me not to use my phone so much.

Q. *Are you addicted to this stuff?*

A. Yeah, I think so. I've developed addictions from time to time to various games on my phone.

Like many of the people in the survey I mentioned earlier, I'm addicted to email. I can't stop checking it. I can't go to bed at night if I haven't cleared my inbox. I'll keep my phone next to my bed, much as I try not to.

The technology is designed to hook us that way. Email is bottomless. Social media platforms are endless. Twitter? The feed never really ends. You could sit there 24 hours a day and you'll never get to the end. And so you come back for more and more.

Q. *If you were advising a friend on quitting their behavioral addictions, what would you suggest?*

A. I'd suggest that they be more mindful about how they are allowing tech to invade their life. Next, they should cordon it off. I like the idea, for instance, of not answering email after six at night.

In general, I'd say find more time to be in natural environments, to sit face to face with someone in a long conversation without any technology in the room. There should be times of the day where it looks like the 1950s or where you are sitting in a room and you can't tell what era you are in. You shouldn't always be looking at screens.

Google Says It Has Found Religion on Privacy

BY DAISUKE WAKABAYASHI AND BRIAN X. CHEN | MAY 7, 2019

MOUNTAIN VIEW, CALIF. — Google, the company that may know the most about our digital lives, is now preaching the gospel of privacy.

Speaking at an annual conference for developers on Tuesday, Sundar Pichai, Google's chief executive, delivered a message that seemed cognizant of today's consumer privacy concerns but out of step with the company's history of intensive online data collection.

"We think privacy is for everyone — not just for the few," Mr. Pichai said. "We want to do more to stay ahead of constantly evolving user expectations."

Google introduced a set of tools spanning a range of its products to provide users with more control over their data and make it more difficult to track their online activities.

Google plans to permit users to navigate its maps, watch videos on YouTube and search for information in "incognito mode," limiting the amount of information shared with the company. It will also allow users to delete web and app activity history automatically after three months or 18 months.

Google added incognito mode to its Chrome browser a decade ago.

The company also said it would make it easier for users to find and delete information they have shared with the company, including location data in maps. For its Android operating system, Google said a new update would simplify how to limit the sharing of location data with app providers.

Last week, Facebook pushed a similar privacy theme at a company conference. Mark Zuckerberg, the company's chief executive, declared that "the future is private" and announced a shift in its products to more intimate communications.

JIM WILSON/THE NEW YORK TIMES

"We think privacy is for everyone — not just for the few," Sundar Pichai, Google's chief executive, said on Tuesday at an annual conference for Google developers.

Google and Facebook have become the dominant forces in online advertising, gobbling up information as their users move around their platforms and the internet at large. But their aggressive collection of user data — laid bare by several embarrassing scandals in recent years — has put the companies in the cross hairs of politicians and global regulators.

While thousands of developers and journalists filed into an outdoor amphitheater where Mr. Pichai delivered his keynote, a plane flew overhead pulling a banner that read: "Google Control Is Not Privacy #savelocalnews."

"I suspect they saw the writing on the wall," said Fatemeh Khatibloo, vice president and principal analyst at Forrester. "These are meaningful changes when it comes to the user's expectations of privacy, but I don't think this affects their business at all. So why shouldn't they do these things to give the impression of more privacy?"

After the keynote speech, Google separately announced it would take steps to limit the use of tracking cookies on Chrome, the world's most popular browser with about a 60 percent market share.

Cookies allow companies to monitor which websites people visit and what ads they have viewed or clicked on. They also are a way for a website to remember who you are so you don't have to log in every time you visit. Cookies level the playing field for smaller companies in the digital advertising world — allowing them to collect information that helps refine ad targeting.

The announcement is another example of a privacy measure that will most likely have a bigger impact on Google's competitors. The internet giant uses cookies but is not dependent on them. It already knows more valuable information such as what users search for, what videos they watch and what apps they've loaded on their phones.

Even as it was addressing some of the perils of data collection, Google demonstrated how it was using information that people provide to the company to make its products more useful.

Its next-generation Assistant, powered by the company's artificial intelligence, can learn more about you to personalize reminders and tasks. It can remember your partner's birthday, for example, and remind you to buy a present a week beforehand. It can also help book car reservations on the web using emails and calendar information.

It can also understand better what you are doing. Google's digital assistant will have a driving mode to help drivers play music, set map destinations or answer phone calls more easily without taking their hands off the wheel.

To make its Assistant faster and more responsive, Google unveiled a change in how the technology works on smartphones. Google said it would start processing what users say to the Assistant on the device — instead of sending it to data centers — allowing the smartphone to respond more quickly.

The company also introduced cheaper versions of its Pixel smartphone, bringing the company's lauded camera technologies to a new audience of budget-conscious consumers. The devices, called Pixel 3A and Pixel 3A XL, start at about $400 and $480, compared to $800 and $900 for their high-end counterparts.

IDC, a research firm, said a sales decline last quarter in the United States was linked to a slowdown for high-end devices, which include iPhones, Samsung Galaxy devices and Google's Pixels.

Though slower and lacking features like wireless-charging and a wide-angle lens, the cheaper Pixel shares many of the same characteristics as Google's premium devices. For one, they include the same rear camera, which includes a mode called Night Sight, which makes photos in low light look like they were taken in normal lighting.

CHAPTER 2

Handheld Wonderland

Smartphones connect people with the Internet and each other in increasingly fast and convenient ways, but they also pose challenges of regulation. Individuals have to monitor and regulate their own use of the devices, and institutions have to address tech-based social issues and determine when to get involved. There are even different apps and other products marketed specifically to help people use their smartphones less. Even though smartphone technology is still relatively young, it has influenced how millions of people interact and function in their everyday lives.

Students Sue Prosecutor in Cellphone Photos Case

BY SEAN D. HAMILL | MARCH 25, 2009

WHEN A HIGH SCHOOL cheerleader in northeastern Pennsylvania learned that she might face criminal charges after investigators reported finding a nude photo of her on someone else's cellphone, she was more confused than frightened at being caught up in a case of "sexting": the increasingly popular phenomenon of nude or seminude photos sent over wireless phones.

"They said they had a full-bodied naked picture of me, but I knew I'd never had any naked picture taken of me," the student, Marissa Miller, 15, recalled of the Feb. 10 telephone call to her mother as the

JESSICA KOURKOUNIS FOR THE NEW YORK TIMES

Marissa Miller and two other Tunkhannock, Pa., high school students say a prosecutor retaliated when they rejected his deal in a case over cellphone photos he called "provocative."

two were having lunch together at Tunkhannock Area High School. Marissa is a freshman at the school, where her mother, MaryJo, works with special education students.

The picture that investigators from the office of District Attorney George P. Skumanick of Wyoming County had was taken two years earlier at a slumber party. It showed Marissa and a friend from the waist up. Both were wearing bras.

Mr. Skumanick said he considered the photo "provocative" enough to tell Marissa and the friend, Grace Kelly, that if they did not attend a 10-hour class dealing with pornography and sexual violence, he was considering filing a charge of sexual abuse of a minor against both girls. If convicted, they could serve time in prison and would probably have to register as sex offenders.

It was the same deal that 17 other students — 13 girls and 4 boys — accepted by the end of February. All of them had either been caught with a cellphone containing pictures of nude or seminude students, or were identified in one or more such photos.

But three students, Marissa, Grace and a third girl who appeared in another photo, along with their mothers, felt the deal was unfair and illegal. On Wednesday, they filed a lawsuit in federal court in Scranton, Pa., against Mr. Skumanick.

They asked the court to stop the district attorney from filing charges against them, contending that his threat to do so was "retaliation" for the families asserting their First and Fourth Amendment rights to oppose his deal.

"Prosecutors should not be using a nuclear-weapon-type charge like child pornography against kids who have no criminal intent and are merely doing stupid things," said Witold J. Walczak, a lawyer with the American Civil Liberties Union of Pennsylvania, which represents the families.

Mr. Skumanick said Wednesday that he would oppose the lawsuit and that he did not consider the deal he offered retaliatory.

"I'm simply giving them an option," said Mr. Skumanick, a Republican who has been district attorney for 20 years and faces re-election again in November. "We're not forcing anybody to do anything. Frankly, it's sad to me that their parents don't realize this is wrong and they should be encouraging them to take the classes."

Almost unheard of a year or two ago, sexting cases are popping up with more frequency across the country.

A survey of 1,280 teenagers and young adults released in December by the National Campaign to Prevent Teenage and Unplanned Pregnancy and CosmoGirl.com found that 20 percent of teenagers and 33 percent of young adults ages 20 to 26 said they had sent or posted nude or seminude photos of themselves.

"Is this today's example of the sky is falling?" said Bill Albert, a spokesman for the campaign, a nonprofit group in Washington. "No, and I don't think we need to overreact."

But since the survey also showed that teenagers who engage in sexting were more likely to have casual sex, Mr. Albert said: "I think it is something else to address and have a conversation about between teens and parents. Is there a role for law enforcement here? That's an open question."

In large part because sexting cases are so new, local communities across the country vary greatly in their handling, from filing child pornography charges against the teenagers involved to alerting parents and letting them deal with it.

Lee Tien, a senior staff lawyer for the Electronic Frontier Foundation, a nonprofit group in San Francisco that studies technology issues, said such cases also raise thorny legal issues around the searching of students' cellphones, many of which are seized when they are used during class.

"If they confiscate the phone, that's reasonable to hold it for the day and return it," Mr. Tien said. "But there's a serious question of whether that justifies going through the cellphone."

The lawsuit filed Wednesday does not address those issues, or the role Tunkhannock Area High School might have played in the investigation, but Mr. Walczak said the A.C.L.U. was "assessing possible legal action against the school."

"Those cellphones contain highly personal information protected by the Fourth Amendment," he said.

A Tunkhannock lawyer, Gerald Grimaud, said a majority of the district's 10-member school board informally supports the increased scrutiny of students' cellphones, but Mr. Grimaud faulted school officials for contacting the district attorney after the first photos were found last fall.

"We're talking about naïve kids getting caught up in these draconian penalties," Mr. Grimaud said. "That seems pretty extreme to me." Other board members did not return calls or could not be reached.

You Love Your iPhone. Literally.

OPINION | BY MARTIN LINDSTROM | SEPT. 30, 2011

WITH APPLE WIDELY expected to release its iPhone 5 on Tuesday, Apple addicts across the world are getting ready for their latest fix.

But should we really characterize the intense consumer devotion to the iPhone as an addiction? A recent experiment that I carried out using neuroimaging technology suggests that drug-related terms like "addiction" and "fix" aren't as scientifically accurate as a word we use to describe our most cherished personal relationships. That word is "love."

As a branding consultant, I have followed Apple from its early days as a cult brand to its position today as one of the most valuable, widely admired companies on earth. A few years back, I conducted an experiment to examine the similarities between some of the world's strongest brands and the world's greatest religions. Using functional magnetic resonance imaging (fMRI) tests, my team looked at subjects' brain activity as they viewed consumer images involving brands like Apple and Harley-Davidson and religious images like rosary beads and a photo of the pope. We found that the brain activity was uncannily similar when viewing both types of imagery.

This past summer, I gathered a group of 20 babies between the ages of 14 and 20 months. I handed each one a BlackBerry. No sooner had the babies grasped the phones than they swiped their little fingers across the screens as if they were iPhones, seemingly expecting the screens to come to life. It appears that a whole new generation is being primed to navigate the world of electronics in a ritualized, Apple-approved way.

Friends who have accidentally left home without their iPhones tell me they feel stressed-out, cut off and somehow un-whole. That sounds a lot like separation anxiety to me. Not long ago, I headed an effort to identify the 10 most powerful, affecting sounds in the world: I found that a vibrating phone came in third, behind only the Intel chime and the sound of a baby giggling. Phantom vibration syndrome is the term I use to describe our habit of scrambling for a cellphone we feel rippling in our pocket, only to find out we are mistaken. Similar to pressing an elevator button repeatedly in the belief that the elevator will descend sooner, we check our phones for e-mails and texts countless times a day, almost as if we can will others to text, call, e-mail or Skype us.

So are our smartphones addictive, medically speaking? Some psychologists suggest that using our iPhones and BlackBerrys may tap into the same associative learning pathways in the brain that make other compulsive behaviors — like gambling — so addictive. As with addiction to drugs or cigarettes or food, the chemical driver of this process is the feel-good neurotransmitter dopamine.

Earlier this year, I carried out an fMRI experiment to find out whether iPhones were really, truly addictive, no less so than alcohol, cocaine, shopping or video games. In conjunction with the San Diego-based firm MindSign Neuromarketing, I enlisted eight men and eight women between the ages of 18 and 25. Our 16 subjects were exposed separately to audio and to video of a ringing and vibrating iPhone.

In each instance, the results showed activation in both the audio and visual cortices of the subjects' brains. In other words, when they were exposed to the video, our subjects' brains didn't just see the vibrating iPhone, they "heard" it, too; and when they were exposed to the audio, they also "saw" it. This powerful cross-sensory phenomenon is known as synesthesia.

But most striking of all was the flurry of activation in the insular cortex of the brain, which is associated with feelings of love and compassion. The subjects' brains responded to the sound of their phones as they would respond to the presence or proximity of a girlfriend, boyfriend or family member.

In short, the subjects didn't demonstrate the classic brain-based signs of addiction. Instead, they *loved* their iPhones.

As we embrace new technology that does everything but kiss us on the mouth, we risk cutting ourselves off from human interaction. For many, the iPhone has become a best friend, partner, lifeline, companion and, yes, even a Valentine. The man or woman we love most may be seated across from us in a romantic Paris bistro, but his or her 8GB, 16GB or 32GB rival lies in wait inside our pockets and purses.

My best advice? Shut off your iPhone, order some good Champagne and find love and compassion the old-fashioned way.

MARTIN LINDSTROM is the author of "Brandwashed: Tricks Companies Use to Manipulate Our Minds and Persuade Us to Buy."

Seeing Social Media More as Portal Than as Pitfall

BY PERRI KLASS, M.D. | JAN. 9, 2012

MORE THAN A hundred years ago, when the telephone was introduced, there was some hand-wringing over the social dangers that this new technology posed: increased sexual aggression and damaged human relationships. "It was going to bring down our society," said Dr. Megan Moreno, a specialist in adolescent medicine at the University of Wisconsin-Madison. "Men would be calling women and making lascivious comments, and women would be so vulnerable, and we'd never have civilized conversations again."

In other words, the telephone provoked many of the same worries that more recently have been expressed about online social media. "When a new technology comes out that is something so important, there is this initial alarmist reaction," Dr. Moreno said.

Indeed, much of the early research — and many of the early pronouncements — on social media seemed calculated to make parents terrified of an emerging technology that many of them did not understand as well as their children did.

Whether about sexting or online bullying or the specter of Internet addiction, "much social media research has been on what people call the danger paradigm," said Dr. Michael Rich, a pediatrician and the director of the Center on Media and Child Health at Children's Hospital Boston.

Though there are certainly real dangers, and though some adolescents appear to be particularly vulnerable, scientists are now turning to a more nuanced understanding of this new world. Many have started to approach social media as an integral, if risky, part of adolescence, perhaps not unlike driving.

Researchers are also looking to Facebook, Twitter and the rest for opportunities to identify problems, to hear cries for help and to provide information and support. Dr. Rich, who sees many teenagers who struggle with Internet-related issues, feels strongly that it is important to avoid blanket judgments about the dangers of going online.

"We should not view social media as either positive or negative, but as essentially neutral," he said. "It's what we do with the tools that decides how they affect us and those around us."

Dr. Moreno's early research looked at adolescents who displayed evidence of risky behaviors on public MySpace profiles, posting photos or statements that referred to sexual activity or substance abuse. E-mails were sent to those adolescents suggesting that they modify their profiles or make them private.

Girls were more likely to respond than boys, Dr. Moreno found, and sexual material was more likely than alcohol-related material to be removed.

Her current research, by contrast, approaches social media as a window, an opportunity to understand and improve both physical and mental health. In a study of the ways college students describe sadness in status updates on their Facebook profiles, she showed that some such expressions were associated with depression in students who completed clinical screening tests.

Since freshman year is a high-risk time for depression, many college resident advisers already try to use Facebook to monitor students, Dr. Moreno said. Perhaps it will be possible to help R.A.'s recognize red flags in the online profiles of their charges.

Still, she acknowledged that this new strategy raised privacy concerns, asking, "How do you think about extending this to other at-risk groups in a way that still doesn't feel like an invasion of privacy?" For example, can we help people in support groups take care of one another better through social media?

Going back and forth, as I do these days, between the worlds of academic pediatrics and academic journalism, I am struck by the focus in both settings on the potential — and the risks — of social media and on the importance of understanding how communication is changing.

JULIETTE BORDA

Our children are using social media to accomplish the eternal goals of adolescent development, which include socializing with peers, investigating the world, trying on identities and establishing independence.

In 2011, the American Academy of Pediatrics Council on Communications and Media issued a clinical report, "The Impact of Social Media on Children, Adolescents and Families." It began by emphasizing the benefits of social media for children and adolescents, including enhanced communication skills and opportunities for social connections.

"A large part of this generation's social and emotional development is occurring while on the Internet and on cellphones," the report noted.

Our job as parents is to help them manage all this wisely, to understand — and avoid — some of the special dangers and consequences of making mistakes in these media. (We can expect the same kind of gratitude that we get for all of our guidance: mixed, of course, with an extra helping of contempt if our technical skills are not up to theirs.)

"Rather than taking a one-size-fits-all harm model, one of the questions parents need to ask is, 'How is this going to interact with my child's personality?' " said Clay Shirky, who teaches about social media at New York University. "Digital media is an amplifier. It tends to make extroverts more extroverted and introverts more introverted."

And both parents and researchers need to be sure they understand the subtleties of the ways teenagers interpret social media.

At a 2011 symposium on the Internet and society, two researchers presented information on how teenagers understand negative talk on the Internet. What adults interpret as bullying is often read by teenagers as "drama," a related but distinct phenomenon.

By understanding how teenagers think about harsh rhetoric, the researchers suggested, we may find ways to help them defend themselves against the real dangers of online aggression.

The problems of cyberbullying and Internet overuse are serious, and the risks of making mistakes online are very real. But even those who treat adolescents with these problems are now committed to the idea that there are other important perspectives for researchers — or parents, or teachers — looking at the brave new universe in which adolescence is taking place.

Social media, said Dr. Rich, "are the new landscape, the new environment in which kids are sorting through the process of becoming autonomous adults — the same things that have been going on since the earth cooled."

You Don't Have to Feel Very Guilty About Using Your Smartphone While Parenting

COLUMN | BY FARHAD MANJOO | JULY 8, 2014

MY 3-YEAR-OLD SON was off from preschool last week, and just between you and me, I played partial hooky from work to take care of him.

I'm asking you to keep it on the down low because as far as my bosses and co-workers are concerned, I've been a busy bee. Last week, like every week, I wrote a column, conducted a half-dozen lengthy interviews, kept up with news about the industry I cover and tweeted obsessively and mercilessly. Also, here I am, writing this post, which is a kind of work, too.

And yet one day last week my son and I spent much of the morning and early afternoon at a science museum. At other times, we played with bubbles and toy woolly mammoths. He served me a baked lemon from his pretend food truck. I got him an ice cream in the park. We participated in a grad student's child-development research study. We visited a construction site.

Sure, he watched some TV, too, and played by himself for a bit. Most of the time, though, there was little sign that I was hard at work.

If you've got kids and an amenable, digital-friendly job, you've most likely performed similar work-life acrobatic feats. These situations come with no small amount of guilt. You worry that while you're trying to do two things at once, you're accomplishing neither. You're juggling work and parenting, and you're inadequate at both.

This is parenting; there's no getting around the guilt. But thanks to technology, I was managing to do a reasonably good job at work while being a fairly adequate parent. It wasn't ideal. But it was probably far better than the alternative, which would be to ship my son off to a nanny or grandparent for the week while I spent all day plugging away at the office, not seeing him.

Technology generally gets a bad parenting rap — particularly smartphones. Every few months, there is a new article voicing concerns about how we're all being terrible parents because we just can't stop staring at our phones. Parental smartphone addiction has also been a rising worry among child-development scholars. The concern is justified; smartphones are changing how we relate to other human beings, so it's reasonable to worry about how they'll affect parenting.

But we rarely consider how, by liberating us from the office, smartphones have greatly expanded the opportunity for certain kinds of workers to increase their involvement in their children's lives. Because you can work from anywhere thanks to your phone, you can be present and at least partly attentive to your children in scenarios where, in the past, you'd have had to be totally absent. Even though my son had to yell for my attention once when I was fixed to my phone, if I didn't have that phone, I would almost certainly not have been able to be with him that day — or at any one of numerous school events or extracurricular activities. I would have been in an office. And he would have been with a caretaker.

That's the trade-off few of us think about when we consider how phones have changed parenting. Before the modern portable office — before the Internet made it possible for a wide variety of workers to work from home, and before smartphones made it possible to work from anywhere — white-collar jobs required a central office. In pre-digital times, the office functioned as a nexus of collaboration and production, and the further you got from the office, the less you got done. So when a child-care emergency popped up, you had to make a choice between work and the child. Or you could try both, to disastrous ends — see Diane Keaton in "Baby Boom."

Much of this is obvious, but we rarely consider the stifling past. Instead, when we think about how our phones intrude on parenting, the primary emotion is crippling guilt. There's an entire online cottage industry devoted to shaming parents whose noses are buried in their devices. Check out the Parents On Phones Tumblr, which features an endless stream of absolutely damning pictures of people ignoring their kids. Its motto is: "Shining a light on the culture of mobile phones and parental neglect."

That's a smug attitude, but I admit I often feel that way. I feel awful when I reach for my phone while I'm with my children. And when I see another parent texting while at the park, I experience a thrilling sense of superiority because my phone is securely in my pocket — at least until it buzzes with an important message, and I pull it out — and ignore the kids while I respond to some supposedly urgent thing.

I feel guilty, but I use my phone anyway. Meanwhile, many of us are tapping away. Researchers at Boston University recently published an anthropological study of smartphone usage among parents. They visited several fast food restaurants, and observed 55 people with children; 40 were using phones. The notes from the study read like a sci-fi hellscape of parental obliviousness:

> *Female caregiver brings food over and sits down across from girl, they distribute the food and as [school aged] girl starts eating caregiver brings out her smartphone. There is no conversation. Caregiver appears to be typing into phone, holding it about 10 inches away from her face, looking into it for long stretches during which she does not look up. She stops typing and is staring at the screen, touching it at points, holding it with her right hand while she leans her chin on her left hand, her facial expression flat. She has been looking at it for about 2 min without any change of gaze, while the girl eats and looks around the room.*

It's a dismaying read. Yet studies like this are incomplete, because they can't address two questions that are central to the debate about smartphones and parenting. First, how attentive would smartphone-distracted parents have been in pre-smartphone times? If we didn't have phones, would we have been paying total attention to our children, or would we have found distraction in books, newspapers, TV or our own heads?

Second, in the absence of phones, how many smartphone-addicted parents would be forced to spend less time with their children because they didn't have the technical capacity to skip out of the office? In the discourse about phones, we often assume that the operative choice, for parents, is between spending non-distracted time with your kids versus distracted time. But it's a tough economy, and jobs are hard to find; if we couldn't work away from the office, wouldn't a lot of us just spend more time at the office?

These questions are difficult to answer. But they're worth considering. For me, it's far too soon to conclude that phones are, on balance, bad for parenting. I spent a lot of quality time with my son last week. He and I had a great time. I also got a lot of work done. And it was all made possible by my phone.

Addicted to Your Phone? There's Help for That

BY CONOR DOUGHERTY | JULY 11, 2015

LIKE PRETTY MUCH EVERYONE these days, Susan Butler stares at her smartphone too much. Unlike most everyone, she took action, buying a $195 ring from a company called Ringly, which promises to "let you put your phone away and your mind at ease."

Ringly does this by connecting its rings to a smartphone filter so that users can silence Gmail or Facebook notifications while preserving crucial alerts, like text messages from a babysitter, which cause the ring to light up or vibrate.

"Hopefully it will keep some distance between my phone and my hand," said Ms. Butler, 27, who lives in Austin, Tex., and is a technology consultant for small businesses.

Given how quickly cellphones have taken over our lives, it's easy to forget that they are still a relatively new technology. The first iPhone came out eight years ago, and today a little more than half the American population has a smartphone, according to eMarketer.

Yet already people spend close to three hours a day looking at a mobile screen — and that excludes the time they spend actually talking on the phones.

In a recent survey of smartphone use by Bank of America, about a third of respondents said they were "constantly" checking their smartphones, and a little more than two-thirds said that they went to bed with a smartphone by their side. Those habits have prompted enough soul searching that a slew of new companies see a business opportunity in helping people cut back.

"Technology has evolved so quickly that we have spiraled out of control and nobody has stopped to think about how this is going to impact our lives," said Kate Unsworth, the founder of a British company, Kovert, that also makes high-tech jewelry to filter out everything but the most urgent stuff.

Many of these distraction-reducing products fall into the growing "wearable technology" niche. Smartwatches like the Apple Watch are designed to encourage more glancing and less phone checking. Last month Google and Levi's announced plans for a line of high-tech clothes that will allow people to do things like turn off a ringing phone by swiping their jacket cuff.

"If there is a chance to enable the clothes that we already love to help us facilitate access to the best and most necessary of this digital world while maintaining eye contact with the person we're eating dinner with, this is a real value," said Paul Dillinger, Levi's head of global product innovation.

An application called Offtime limits customers' access to apps they overuse and logs their activity to produce charts on how much time they spend on their phones. Another, called Moment, encourages people to share their phone use with friends to compete in a game of who can look at their phone the least. And a New York designer recently completed a crowdfunding campaign for the Light Phone, a credit-card-size phone that does nothing but make and receive phone calls and "is designed to be used as little as possible."

Perhaps most radical is the NoPhone, a $12 piece of plastic that looks like a smartphone but actually does nothing. Van Gould, an art director at a New York advertising agency who moonlights as head of the nascent venture, said he and his partners had sold close to 3,200 NoPhones, which they market as a security blanket for people who want to curb their phone addiction but are afraid to leave home without something to hold on to.

Even though many are doubtless bought as gags, "Most people don't think about phone addiction as a real thing until you're like, 'O.K., they're buying a piece of plastic because they are worried about their friend,' " Mr. Gould said.

MATTHIEU BOUREL

Adam Gazzaley, a neurologist and neuroscience professor at the University of California, San Francisco, said, "You have a population that is starting to say, 'Wait, we love all this technology but there seems to be a cost — whether it's my relationship or my work or my safety because I'm driving and texting.' "

In the days before apps, you searched online when you wanted something, and that was that. But now that the Internet is increasingly mobile and companies are more sophisticated about tracking users' history and preferences, technology is less about "pulling," through Google searches, and more about "pushing," through smartphone notifications that are impossible to ignore because they cause our phones to light up and go ding.

Some products are trying to find a balance, like Google Now, a kind of digital assistant that uses data like location, Gmails and browsing activity to predict what a user might want next. Part of the idea is to bother you only when you need it. "If I'm about to forget my kid's birthday I want the phone to scream at me until I do something about it," said Sundar Pichai, Google's senior vice president of products.

This also makes business sense. The more people trust Google to navigate their lives, the more they'll use apps like Google Calendar and Gmail. And the more Google understands its users, the more it can fine-tune its advertising engine.

Mr. Pichai's philosophy is to give people lots of choices and let them figure it out by themselves. "We need to design products which are genuinely centered around users," Mr. Pichai said, "and then there is a line by which users choose to live their lives. It's their choice, and I want to be careful not to be prescriptive."

But smartphones are a potent delivery mechanism for two fundamental human impulses, according to Paul Atchley, a psychology professor at the University of Kansas: our quest to find new and interesting distractions, and our desire to feel that we have checked off a task.

"With these devices you can get that sense of accomplishment multiple times a minute," he said. "The brain gets literally rewired to switch — to constantly seek out novelty, which makes putting the phone down difficult."

Like many of us, when Ms. Butler comes out of a meeting or a doctor's appointment, she finds herself craving social media updates. She also had a nagging habit of opening a website, closing it, then opening it right back up in the hope that something new would appear. Addiction or not, it was enough for her to seek help from Ringly.

Mr. Atchley, for one, is skeptical. Addiction is an intensely personal matter, he said, and successful treatment is about having the resolve to control our demons — not outsourcing them to message filters.

In technology, as in life, a little willpower goes a long way.

CONOR DOUGHERTY is a technology reporter for The New York Times.

Addicted to Your Smartphone? The Company That Made It Would Like You to Think So.

BY JONAH ENGEL BROMWICH | JULY 30, 2015

WHO IS MAKING the most noise about smartphone overuse? It seems that it might be smartphone companies themselves.

A survey released this week by Motorola tried to illustrate that people around the world are obsessed with smartphones. A recent report from Ericsson also emphasized the amount of time certain users are spending on their phones.

Even the company that popularized the smartphone is expressing concern for its customers. In an interview with Wired earlier this year, Kevin Lynch, the man responsible for developing the software for the Apple Watch, seemed concerned about our inability to detach:

"We're so connected, kind of ever-presently, with technology now," Mr. Lynch said. "People are carrying their phones with them and looking at the screen so much."

We asked Brian X. Chen, The Times's consumer technology expert and the author of a book about constant connectivity, "Always On," to explain why smartphone companies are so interested in what their products are doing to us. He said that because consumer anxiety about overusing smartphones has lessened, companies feel more comfortable using that line of thinking as a way to market new products.

Q. *Why are all these studies coming out about smartphone addiction? Do you think it's something that people are worried about?*

A. I think Microsoft and Nokia tried to do this in 2010. They had all these ads come out that said the Windows phone is better than iPhone because it helps you get away from your phone more. We made this more streamlined, more efficient and easier to use, so therefore, you're going to spend less time on your smartphone. Which, you know, just didn't turn out to be true. It was just a marketing twist, and we're seeing more of that now.

Q. *But there are definitely people who are anxious about using their smartphones too much. Do you think those people are addicted? Are there legitimate worries about using our phones too much?*

A. It's a case-by-case basis, but there are legitimate concerns for people and their everyday interactions. It's generally rude to keep looking at your smartphone when you're at dinner with your friends, for example. When you're in a relationship, and you're spending more time with your smartphone than you are with your partner, then you probably have a problem. So I think those are some of the concerns when it comes to our social relationships.

Q. *Have you ever had anyone complain to you that you're on your phone too much?*

A. I get more of the criticism for video games. But yes, there are technology issues that come up in my life. I'm addicted to email probably, working at The New York Times where our bosses are just emailing us all day. I kind of have to tell myself to get away from that on the weekend and set my own limitations and restrictions.

Q. *How would you suggest people stay away from their phones?*

A. The way that I've set it up is I only get sound for emails when I get emails from my bosses, and I use the V.I.P. alerts on the iPhone. I pretty much ignore everything else, unless it's friends. I turn on "Do Not Disturb" every day from midnight to 6 a.m. just so I'm not getting crazy email noises while we're sleeping.

An argument I make in the book is, simply, if it's really becoming a problem, you can start setting restrictions around yourself. For example, at dinner turn on airplane mode on the iPhone. And stop looking at your phone; pay attention to your partner and your friends and so on. You can do these things!

Q. *The MIT Technology Review had a report a couple of years ago that claimed that smartphones had spread with "unprecedented speed." Do you think the speed of adoption has contributed to the anxiety?*

A. I kind of feel like the opposite: The fact that smartphone adoption is spreading so quickly is kind of proof that people are getting past that anxiety. Back when the smartphone was still becoming a mainstream thing, that's when anxiety was at its peak. But there have been very few studies suggesting anything severely negative about using smartphones.

There has always been fear of new technology. The classic example is that Aristotle warned that using the pen to write would make us stop memorizing things, and that certainly turned out not to be true. And then there's the television. The television is funny in that we've all moved on, but that's one piece of technology that we should actually be more concerned about because it involves a lot of sitting around. And sitting is really, really bad for you.

Sext and the Single Girl

REVIEW | BY CINDI LEIVE | MARCH 23, 2016

GIRLS AND SEX
Navigating the Complicated New Landscape
By Peggy Orenstein
303 pp. Harper. $26.99.

THERE'S A MOMENT midway through Peggy Orenstein's latest book that seems to sum up what it's like to be a teenage girl right now. An economics major taking a gender studies class is getting dressed in her college dorm room for a night out, cheerfully discussing sexual stereotyping in advertising with Orenstein — while at the same time grabbing a miniskirt and a bottle of vodka, the better to achieve her evening goal: to "get really drunk and make out with someone." "You look hot," her friend tells her — and the student, apparently registering the oddness of the scene, turns to Orenstein. "In my gender class I'm all, 'That damned patriarchy,'" she says. "But . . . what's the point of a night if you aren't getting attention from guys?" Her ambition, she explains, "is to be just slutty enough, where you're not a prude but you're not a whore. . . . Finding that balance is every college girl's dream, you know what I mean?"

Exactly how that got to be anyone's dream is the subject of "Girls and Sex," a thought-provoking if occasionally hand-wringing investigation by Orenstein, who in previous books has put classroom sexism, princess obsessions and other phenomena under her microscope. Be warned: Orenstein, a contributing writer for The New York Times Magazine and the mother of a preteen girl, begins her reporting worried by what she's heard about "hookup culture" — and ends it even more freaked out. It's not that girls are having so much sex (the percentage of high-schoolers who have had intercourse is actually dropping); even if they were, Orenstein's careful to say she wouldn't judge, really. But the acts the girls are engaging in, from oral sex to sexting, tend to be staged, she argues, more for boys' enjoyment than their own. For guys, she says, there is fun and pleasure; for girls (at least the straight ones), too little physical joy, too much regret and a general sense that the boys are in charge. Fully half the girls in Orenstein's book say they've been coerced into sex, and many had been raped — among them, by the way, that econ major, who was so confused that when her assailant dropped her off the next morning, she told him, "Thanks, I had fun." The sexual playing field Orenstein describes is so tilted no girl could win.

I know, I know: Every generation thinks things have gotten more complicated since they were young (it's one of those universally accepted parental truths, like the fact that kids don't go outside and play anymore). But the interesting question at the heart of "Girls and Sex" is not really whether things are better or worse for girls. It's why — at a time when women graduate from college at higher rates than men and are closing the wage gap — aren't young women more satisfied with their most intimate relationships? "When so much has changed for girls in the public realm," Orenstein writes, "why hasn't more . . . changed in the private one?"

To answer this question, Orenstein interviews more than 70 young women between the ages of 15 and 20. Some of the culprits she locates are more familiar than others: There's pornography, which teaches boys to expect constantly willing, fully waxed partners, and girls to imitate all those arched backs and movie-perfect moans. (Sorry, male college students, but studies show that the percentage of your female peers who fake orgasm has been steadily rising.) There are the abstinence-only sex-ed programs of the last two decades, which she argues encourage shame and misinformation; and the unhelpful tendency of even liberal parents to go mute with their daughters on the subject of what they deserve in bed. ("Once parents stopped saying 'Don't,'" Orenstein observes, "many didn't know what to say.") There's alcohol, so much alcohol, a judgment-dulling menu of Jäger bombs and tequila shots. There's selfie culture, which Orenstein charges encourages girls to see themselves as objects to be "liked" (or not) — a simple-sounding phenomenon with surprisingly profound implications, since self-objectification has been linked with everything from depression to risky sexual behavior. There are the constant images of naked, writhing women, as well as the idea that taking your clothes off is a sign of power. ("I love Beyoncé," one girl tells Orenstein. "She's, like, a queen. But I wonder, if she wasn't so beautiful, if people didn't think she was so sexy, would she be able to make the feminist points she makes?") And despite all the time girls spend "impersonating sexiness," Orenstein finds that absent from their universe is a sense of actual female sexuality — figuring out what you want and doing it. Society is giving girls, she concludes, a "psychological clitoridectomy."

Oh, but just one thing — plenty of the girls Orenstein interviews don't see it that way at all, and it's to her credit that she documents them pushing back against what they view as her old-school assumptions. (No, they tell her, Nicki Minaj isn't a sex object — she's a self-determining superstar.) These conversations are the most interesting, least expected part of "Girls and Sex," as when girls share that while an endless string of hookups can bum them out, many of them prefer it to "catching feelings" for a guy, which would make them more vulnerable. (The interviews also reveal an almost comical generation gap. When one recent high school graduate explains to Orenstein that performing oral sex is "like money or some kind of currency. … It's how you make friends with the popular guys. … It's more impersonal than sex," Orenstein writes, "I may be of a different generation, but, frankly, it's hard for me to consider a penis in my mouth as 'impersonal.'")

It's a laugh-out-loud line, but Orenstein is of a different generation, and teenagers themselves may bristle at her judgment of them as victims. When she attends a Miley Cyrus concert and dismisses the half-naked star as "the opposite" of "unique," and a "lint trap of images and ideas," you know what she means — but that lint trap is also an actual young woman who is working out many of the same issues facing Orenstein's subjects (a fact that surely accounts for some of her popularity: "Slut-shamed" after her romp with Robin Thicke on the MTV Video Music Awards, Cyrus has held her own — a teen-girl revenge fantasy). What's more, the real-life teenage world isn't all Kardashians, anyway: Celebrities like Lorde have become popular without embracing the sex-doll style Orenstein frets over; thrift-shop dresses and Converse high-tops now mingle with minis and stilettos in teenage closets everywhere; even the Pirelli calendar dumped its nude models this year for shots of high-achieving women like the young blogger Tavi Gevinson, clothed. When Kim Kardashian tweeted a nude selfie recently, sure, some young women cheered her on — but plenty posted the Twitter version of an eye-roll. The truth is, female culture is more varied and rebellious than "Girls and Sex" lets on.

And "Girls and Sex" isn't really about all girls: Though gay teenagers are included (and seem generally happier in their relationships than their straight peers), Orenstein's interviewees are mostly upper-middle-class, and she is mainly concerned with sex's impact on their emotional lives, not physical well-being — pregnancy and S.T.D.s come up rarely in her interviews, and current-day abortion access not at all. But given that low-income young women are less able to pay, say, to travel across state lines to an open abortion clinic, you wonder how the picture of sex and its implications would have looked if girls of all incomes had been included. A bad night is one thing; a baby at 17 is another.

At any rate, the true audience for "Girls and Sex" isn't girls at all — but parents trying to understand them. So what should a mother or father hoping for a sexually well-adjusted daughter do? "Here's a solution," Orenstein offers, only somewhat in jest. "Move to the Netherlands." Dutch girls, she points out, are more likely to have sex in the context of loving relationships, and less because of boys' expectations, than here at home. There are useful lessons from the Dutch examples: Parents and teachers there, she explains, talk to kids about sex — not just the birds and bees and condoms, but also pleasure and consent and exactly how to say no, or yes; they even endorse in-home sleepovers versus sneaking around. Orenstein makes an excellent case that all this will help (though it may not be easy: My own 13-year-old bolted from the room every time I tried to talk about this book with her and is probably in Nebraska by now). But the sweeping issues her reporting illuminates clearly can't be solved by dinner-table or classroom conversations alone.

To really fix things, you'll need bigger solutions, and it's tempting to wish Orenstein would put down her reporter's notebook to write a more focused sexual bill of rights that girls themselves, and not just their parents, can get behind. "Girls and Sex" is full of thoughtful concern and empathetic questions: What if girls learned that their sex drives mattered as much as boys'? What if hookups took place sober? What if? But Orenstein is uniquely positioned to do more than ask questions; you want her next book to tell us: Here's how. Let's go.

CINDI LEIVE is the editor in chief of Glamour.

Hooked on Our Smartphones

COLUMN | BY JANE E. BRODY | JAN. 9, 2017

THE MANY MEN, women and children who spend their days glued to their smartphones and social media accounts might learn something from Lin-Manuel Miranda, creator of the groundbreaking megahit "Hamilton." Asked in an interview with Delta Sky magazine when and where he finds time to be creative, Mr. Miranda, an avid reader of books and enthusiast for unfettered downtime, replied: "The good idea comes in the moment of rest. It comes in the shower. It comes when you're doodling or playing trains with your son. 'Hamilton' forced me to double down on being awake to the inspirations of just living my life."

Mr. Miranda's observation bodes ill for the future, not just of creativity but also of healthy bodies, minds and relationships. No doubt you've seen the following scenarios, probably many times:

• Young couples out to dinner pull out their smartphones to check messages, emails and social networks even before scanning the menu, and check their phones repeatedly throughout the meal.

• Shoppers and commuters standing in line, people crossing busy streets, even cyclists and drivers whose eyes are on their phones instead of their surroundings.

• Toddlers in strollers playing with a digital device — a parent's or perhaps even their own — instead of observing and learning from the world around them.

• People walking down the street with eyes on their phones, bumping into others, tripping over or crashing into obstacles.

Observations like these have prompted a New York psychotherapist to ask, "What really matters?" in life. In her enlightening new book, "The Power of Off," Nancy Colier observes that "we are spending far too much of our time doing things that don't really matter to us." Both in and outside her practice, she has encountered many people who have become "disconnected from what really matters, from what makes us feel nourished and grounded as human beings."

The near-universal access to digital technology, starting at ever younger ages, is transforming modern society in ways that can have negative effects on physical and mental health, neurological development and personal relationships, not to mention safety on our roads and sidewalks.

Don't get me wrong. I'm no Luddite. I love technology. I love the convenience and assistance afforded by the myriad apps on my cellphone, a pocket-size information bank. I remember being amazed, as a Times reporter back in the early 1980s, when I started using word processing and realized how much faster I could write an article. Now computers save tons of time and effort and avert countless embarrassing errors because I can look up facts, figures, spelling, definitions and scholarly publications without leaving my ergonomic chair.

But I also love putting my computer in sleep mode and going for a walk with my dog, meeting and chatting with friends, acquaintances and strangers, some of whom have become friends.

As with so much else in life, moderation in our digital world should be the hallmark of a healthy relationship with technology. Too many of us have become slaves to the devices that were supposed to free us, giving us more time to experience life and the people we love. Instead, we're constantly bombarded by bells, buzzes and chimes that alert us to messages we feel compelled to view and respond to immediately.

"Most people now check their smartphones 150 times per day, or every six minutes," Ms. Colier wrote. "And young adults are now sending an average of 110 texts per day." Furthermore, she added, "46 percent of smartphone users now say that their devices are something they 'couldn't live without.' "

In "The World Unplugged Project," investigators at the University of Maryland reported that "a clear majority" of students in the 10

PAUL ROGERS

countries studied experienced distress when they tried to go without their devices for 24 hours. One in three people admitted they'd rather give up sex than their smartphones.

I fear we are turning into digital robots. Will future generations know how to converse with one another face to face? Will they notice the birds, trees, sunrise and the people with whom they share the planet?

Instead of visiting art galleries, attending concerts or walking on picturesque wooded paths, one woman I know who came to Woodstock, N.Y., last summer spent the weekend on her iPad communing with her many "friends" on Facebook. All I could think was "What a waste!"

Why, you may ask, is it so important to limit our digital lives? "Without open spaces and downtime, the nervous system never shuts down — it's in constant fight-or-flight mode," Ms. Colier said in an interview. "We're wired and tired all the time. Even computers reboot, but we're not doing it."

She continued, "It's connections to other human beings — real-life connections, not digital ones — that nourish us and make us feel like we count. Our presence, our full attention is the most important thing we can give each other. Digital communications don't result in deeper connections, in feeling loved and supported."

How often is your real work interrupted by signals from your smartphone that you find impossible to ignore? Have you ever avoided intimacy with your partner because you're in the midst of iPhone Scrabble? Is endlessly snapping selfies and posting your every action and thought on social media creating an unhealthy self-centeredness?

As for physical well-being, every hour spent on a device is likely to be an indoor, sedentary one. Screens are stealing time that children and adolescents should be spending on physical activity and sports, reading, or creating and engaging directly with other children, all of which are critical to healthy physical and social development.

"Children who overuse online media are at risk of problematic internet use, and heavy users of video games are at risk of internet gaming disorder" (translation: addiction), the American Academy of Pediatrics wrote in its latest policy statement on media use.

Ms. Colier, a licensed clinical social worker, said, "The only difference between digital addiction and other addictions is that this is a socially condoned behavior." While her book contains a 30-day digital detox program, in our interview she offered three steps to help curb one's digital dependence.

1. Start by recognizing how much digital use is really needed, say, for work or navigation or letting family members know you're O.K., and what is merely a habit of responding, posting and self-distraction.

2. Make little changes. Refrain from using your device while eating or spending time with friends, and add one thing a day that's done without the phone.

3. Become very conscious of what is important to you, what really nourishes you, and devote more time and attention to it.

Read This. Then Put Away Your Phone.

BY TALYA MINSBERG | MARCH 1, 2019

HALF MOON BAY, CALIF. — See if you can get to the end of this article without being interrupted by another piece of technology

Tristan Harris, a former Google executive, said it could be a challenge, and he compared phones and apps to slot machines that command attention and endlessly distract.

In an unusual twist, Mr. Harris discussed electronic addiction at the recent New York Times New Work Summit on a stage set with candles, as the electricity in the Half Moon Bay area had gone out.

When Mr. Harris worked at Google in 2013, he created a 141-page slide show that acted as a reckoning for the internet giant. What was first shared with around 10 colleagues was later viewed by tens of thousands of employees and others.

"Never before in history have the decisions of a handful of designers (mostly men, white, living in SF, aged 25-35) working at 3 companies (Google, Apple, Facebook) had so much impact on how millions of people around the world spend their attention," the slide show read.

"Think about that for a second," he wrote. "We should feel an enormous responsibility to get this right."

Seven years later, worries about the addictive nature of technology have multiplied. Apple and Google have introduced tools to try to help people better understand, and curb, their technology use.

Top executives in Silicon Valley are increasingly voicing their concerns about technology's influence on young minds. Apple's Timothy D. Cook told The Guardian he didn't want his nephew on any social platforms. Steve Jobs didn't want his children near iPads. Some parents are asking nannies to shield children from their phones.

"Compared to 20 or 30 years ago, technology is eating up every single area of public life," Mr. Harris said in a conversation with Meredith Whittaker of the AI Now Institute and the reporter Nellie Bowles of The Times. "From our elections, to our media, to our culture, to our public sphere, to our conversations, to our children's development — these are all areas of life that technology has gobbled up."

In 2016, he left Google to become a co-founder and the executive director of what is now known as the Center for Humane Technology, an organization that is calling for companies to build systems and business models "that more deeply align with our humanity and how we want to live."

Mr. Harris and Ms. Whittaker say the onus to create meaningful change in the technology world must come from within and outside of companies like Apple, Facebook, Google that have a large hand in creating the expanding attention crisis.

As the lead of Google's Open Research group and an A.I. researcher at New York University, Ms. Whittaker has a unique perspective on the issues and how they could be solved from within and beyond Silicon Valley.

"People are recognizing that there are issues, and they want to change it," Ms. Whittaker said. "But has the objective function of these corporations changed? They're still major corporations at a time of neoliberal capitalism that are optimizing their products for shareholder value."

She continued to say that users and employees must demand accountability. But government regulation is also overdue, she said.

"We need regulation," she said. "Make them open up trade secrecy provisions so we can audit these systems when they are used in public life."

Ms. Whittaker proposed those regulations as part of the 2018 AI Now Report released by New York University in December. "Government regulation is an important component," according to the report, "but leading companies in the A.I. industry also need internal accountability structures that go beyond ethics guidelines."

MIKE COHEN FOR THE NEW YORK TIMES

Meredith Whittaker of the AI Now Institute, left, and Tristan Harris of the Center for Humane Technology discussed electronic addiction at the New Work Summit.

Ms. Whittaker and Mr. Harris said they believed employees within the tech industry want to see specific guidelines put in place.

"We have allies throughout the whole industry because no one wants bad outcomes," Mr. Harris said. No one wants to contribute to a system in which children have poor mental health, he added. "No one wants to contribute to a system where you destabilize democracies or cause genocides across the world."

Once employees see how the current structures can lead to such problems, they ask one question, he said: "How can I help?"

CHAPTER 3

Dangers for Young and Old

People increasingly spend their time on smartphones, tablets, laptops and desktop computers. Games like Age of Empires and Fortnite have grown in popularity, especially among young people. Problems crop up in the home due to overuse of tech, from marital problems to a reduced amount of family time without the interference and distraction of the Internet. Distracted driving causes traffic accidents and fatalities as people are warned about using electronic devices while operating vehicles. Local and state governments have passed laws and regulations prohibiting such uses.

When Love Turns to Obsession, Games Are No Game

BY MICHEL MARRIOTT | MARCH 12, 1998

A MIDDLE-AGED MAN recently sat in his high-rise apartment in Manhattan and commanded ancient Grecian fields to bring forth hunters, miners, builders and soldiers. Soon there were fortresses and armies to storm them. A short time later came the inevitable carnage — flaming ramparts and rotting bodies — that wars have wrought through the ages.

This warfare was strictly play, all part of a popular computer strategy game called Age of Empires. The player, a small-business owner, was battling not only to win the game but to win a contest within himself. He is obsessed, he said, with playing war strategy games on his computer.

"There is a compulsion to play the game over and over until you win," said the man, who spoke on the condition that his name not be used to protect his reputation with clients who would not understand his fixation.

He has taken part in death matches that have started around 10 P.M. and lasted until 3 the next morning. "That's without getting up to get a glass of water, anything to eat or going to the bathroom," he said. "The game totally absorbs you."

Many experts on obsessive behavior agree that there are striking similarities between addictions to substances like drugs and food and addictions to activities like gambling, shopping, sex and computer games. Some addiction counselors have begun to focus on compulsive game players.

But help, addiction experts say, seldom means giving up the games or computers. A common approach to treating computer game addicts is to try to teach them moderation, said Peggy Reynolds, a professor of human development counseling at Vanderbilt University in Nashville.

"You can't go cold turkey," said Dr. Reynolds, explaining that asking a compulsive game player to quit would be like asking an overeater to stop eating. "Computers have become part of our life style. People have to know how to manage them."

"It is addictive," said Monty Smith, a 23-year-old Brooklyn chef who calls himself an obsessive home computer game player. "It can be like a drug."

The business owner said it did not matter whether the games, which usually cost about $50, were set in early southern Europe or on mechanized fantasy planets whirling deep in space. What matters is that they be intellectually engaging.

"I have the need to win," the man said. "I feel like I have to overcome the forces that the computer is throwing against me."

A 35-year-old woman, who asked not to be identified to protect her husband's identity, said she had become alarmed by her husband's nightly marathon playing of computer shoot'em-ups like Doom and Quake. She called the games "electronic crack."

Maressa Hecht Orzack, founder and coordinator of computer addiction services at McLean Hospital in Belmont, Mass., one of the few programs that specifically treats computer game addiction, said she had recently spoken with a drug user who plays computer games. "He said the games gave him the same kind of feeling he got when he was on amphetamines," she said.

Many of these players may be in denial, she added. "The wives of these men, their companions, are the ones who often finger this," Dr. Orzack said.

In the early 1980's, teen-agers and young adults troubled their parents by obsessively playing coin-operated computer games in arcades. Dr. Orzack said that today, many of her patients who considered themselves home computer game addicts were in their 40's, 50's or older. Almost all are men.

Because computer game addiction is relatively new, there are no reliable statistics on the depth of the problem, Dr. Orzack said. She often learns of a game addiction, she said, after it has caused problems with someone's job or marriage.

That is not surprising, said Dr. William S. Pollack, a psychiatrist who is the director of the Center for Men at McLean Hospital, which is affiliated with Harvard Medical School. He said addicts were often dodging things like job worries and marital disputes.

"What lies behind the fascination with the games is ancient," he said. "The games are a new symptomatic way of expressing an old problem: midlife dissatisfaction."

"For some, their dreams of what life would be like when they were 45 or 55 were not coming true," Dr. Pollack said. "They are looking for alternatives, something to take away the pain."

Playing a sophisticated computer game, especially in a darkened den, is an isolating behavior, said Dr. Reynolds, of Vanderbilt. She said men were especially vulnerable to isolating experiences like playing computer games because they were generally less comfortable than women in social settings.

"Playing computer games can be a way of isolating from the stress of being in a relationship, either with the people in the home or in a given community," Dr. Reynolds said.

The middle-aged game player who asked not to be identified said that after years of excessive use of computer games, he had begun preferring to stay at home alone with his games rather than venturing out. "It was easier to stay in with the game than to go out and look for a girlfriend," he said.

He began seeing life lessons in the games, like the critical importance of marshaling resources, he said. Yet he also came to see, he said, that the "games are not life, only imitations of life" and that being with people was what mattered the most.

But John Uppendahl, director of communications for Cavedog Entertainment — the company, based in Woodinville, Wash., near Seattle, that designed Total Annihilation — questioned the concern over computer games. He said worrying about computer game players struck him as ironic in America, a country founded on principles of personal freedom and the pursuit of happiness.

"Unless you're going out and hurting other people, or doing bad things, what's wrong with somebody doing something that they get enjoyment from?" he asked.

While Dr. Pollack cautions men against excessive computer game playing, he does say that becoming immersed in a computer game can have positive effects.

"As they grow older, men get pushed away from play and playfulness," Dr. Pollack said. "They may engage in sport, but that is more about competition and winning and gives men very little chance to just play."

An important factor in keeping game playing from becoming addictive, Dr. Pollack and Dr. Orzack said, is to involve other people in the games.

Ulysses Hill, called Chickie, shrugged his shoulders at that idea. His wife, Nancy, said he had never asked her to join him in his frequent sorties over the Persian Gulf in Jet Fighter III, a computer flight-simulation game that involves combat missions.

"I fly to Iraq every day and sometimes in the middle of the night," said Mr. Hill, who is 62 and is a boxing judge for the International Boxing Federation.

He brushed away any suggestion that his love of his computer game had anything to do with addiction. After five years of flying virtual jets, he said, he could actually fly a F-22 if he had to in a pinch.

"He enjoys it, and I'm fine with that," Mrs. Hill said, calling the game a "stress buster" for her husband.

ADDICTED TO BATTLE

A number of psychological and physical symptoms could well suggest an addiction to computer games, experts say. Here are some symptoms compiled by Maressa Hecht Orzack, founder and coordinator of computer addiction services at McLean Hospital in Belmont, Mass.

THE PSYCHOLOGICAL SYMPTOMS

- Having a sense of power and euphoria while playing the game.
- Being unable to stop playing.
- Craving more and more time playing the game.
- Neglecting family, friends and social activities.
- Feeling empty, depressed and irritable when not playing.
- Lying about game playing.
- Having school or job problems.

SOME PHYSICAL SYMPTOMS

- Repetitive stress disorders.
- Dry eyes and migraine headaches.
- Backaches.
- Eating irregularities, like skipping a meal.
- Lapse in personal hygiene.
- Sleep disturbances.

Attached to Technology and Paying a Price

BY MATT RICHTEL | JUNE 6, 2010

SAN FRANCISCO — When one of the most important e-mail messages of his life landed in his in-box a few years ago, Kord Campbell overlooked it.

Not just for a day or two, but 12 days. He finally saw it while sifting through old messages: a big company wanted to buy his Internet start-up.

"I stood up from my desk and said, 'Oh my God, oh my God, oh my God,' " Mr. Campbell said. "It's kind of hard to miss an e-mail like that, but I did."

The message had slipped by him amid an electronic flood: two computer screens alive with e-mail, instant messages, online chats, a Web browser and the computer code he was writing.

While he managed to salvage the $1.3 million deal after apologizing to his suitor, Mr. Campbell continues to struggle with the effects of the deluge of data. Even after he unplugs, he craves the stimulation he gets from his electronic gadgets. He forgets things like dinner plans, and he has trouble focusing on his family.

His wife, Brenda, complains, "It seems like he can no longer be fully in the moment."

This is your brain on computers.

Scientists say juggling e-mail, phone calls and other incoming information can change how people think and behave. They say our ability to focus is being undermined by bursts of information.

These play to a primitive impulse to respond to immediate opportunities and threats. The stimulation provokes excitement — a dopamine squirt — that researchers say can be addictive. In its absence, people feel bored.

The resulting distractions can have deadly consequences, as when cellphone-wielding drivers and train engineers cause wrecks. And for millions of people like Mr. Campbell, these urges can inflict nicks and cuts on creativity and deep thought, interrupting work and family life.

While many people say multitasking makes them more productive, research shows otherwise. Heavy multitaskers actually have more trouble focusing and shutting out irrelevant information, scientists say, and they experience more stress.

And scientists are discovering that even after the multitasking ends, fractured thinking and lack of focus persist. In other words, this is also your brain *off* computers.

"The technology is rewiring our brains," said Nora Volkow, director of the National Institute of Drug Abuse and one of the world's leading brain scientists. She and other researchers compare the lure of digital stimulation less to that of drugs and alcohol than to food and sex, which are essential but counterproductive in excess.

Technology use can benefit the brain in some ways, researchers say. Imaging studies show the brains of Internet users become more efficient at finding information. And players of some video games develop better visual acuity.

More broadly, cellphones and computers have transformed life. They let people escape their cubicles and work anywhere. They shrink distances and handle countless mundane tasks, freeing up time for more exciting pursuits.

For better or worse, the consumption of media, as varied as e-mail and TV, has exploded. In 2008, people consumed three times as much information each day as they did in 1960. And they are constantly shifting their attention. Computer users at work change windows or check e-mail or other programs nearly 37 times an hour, new research shows.

The nonstop interactivity is one of the most significant shifts ever in the human environment, said Adam Gazzaley, a neuroscientist at the University of California, San Francisco.

"We are exposing our brains to an environment and asking them to do things we weren't necessarily evolved to do," he said. "We know already there are consequences."

Mr. Campbell, 43, came of age with the personal computer, and he is a heavier user of technology than most. But researchers say the habits and struggles of Mr. Campbell and his family typify what many experience — and what many more will, if trends continue.

For him, the tensions feel increasingly acute, and the effects harder to shake.

The Campbells recently moved to California from Oklahoma to start a software venture. Mr. Campbell's life revolves around computers.

He goes to sleep with a laptop or iPhone on his chest, and when he wakes, he goes online. He and Mrs. Campbell, 39, head to the tidy kitchen in their four-bedroom hillside rental in Orinda, an affluent suburb of San Francisco, where she makes breakfast and watches a TV news feed in the corner of the computer screen while he uses the rest of the monitor to check his e-mail.

Major spats have arisen because Mr. Campbell escapes into video games during tough emotional stretches. On family vacations, he has trouble putting down his devices. When he rides the subway to San Francisco, he knows he will be offline 221 seconds as the train goes through a tunnel.

Their 16-year-old son, Connor, tall and polite like his father, recently received his first C's, which his family blames on distraction from his gadgets. Their 8-year-old daughter, Lily, like her mother, playfully tells her father that he favors technology over family.

"I would love for him to totally unplug, to be totally engaged," says Mrs. Campbell, who adds that he becomes "crotchety until he gets his fix." But she would not try to force a change.

"He loves it. Technology is part of the fabric of who he is," she says. "If I hated technology, I'd be hating him, and a part of who my son is too."

ALWAYS ON

Mr. Campbell, whose given name is Thomas, had an early start with technology in Oklahoma City. When he was in third grade, his parents bought him Pong, a video game. Then came a string of game consoles and PCs, which he learned to program.

In high school, he balanced computers, basketball and a romance with Brenda, a cheerleader with a gorgeous singing voice. He studied too, with focus, uninterrupted by e-mail. "I did my homework because I needed to get it done," he said. "I didn't have anything else to do."

He left college to help with a family business, then set up a lawn mowing service. At night he would read, play video games, hang out with Brenda and, as she remembers it, "talk a lot more."

In 1996, he started a successful Internet provider. Then he built the start-up that he sold for $1.3 million in 2003 to LookSmart, a search engine.

Mr. Campbell loves the rush of modern life and keeping up with the latest information. "I want to be the first to hear when the aliens land," he said, laughing. But other times, he fantasizes about living in pioneer days when things moved more slowly: "I can't keep everything in my head."

No wonder. As he came of age, so did a new era of data and communication.

At home, people consume 12 hours of media a day on average, when an hour spent with, say, the Internet and TV simultaneously counts as two hours. That compares with five hours in 1960, say researchers at the University of California, San Diego. Computer users visit an average of 40 Web sites a day, according to research by RescueTime, which offers time-management tools.

As computers have changed, so has the understanding of the human brain. Until 15 years ago, scientists thought the brain stopped developing after childhood. Now they understand that its neural networks continue to develop, influenced by things like learning skills.

So not long after Eyal Ophir arrived at Stanford in 2004, he wondered whether heavy multitasking might be leading to changes in a characteristic of the brain long thought immutable: that humans can process only a single stream of information at a time.

Going back a half-century, tests had shown that the brain could barely process two streams, and could not simultaneously make decisions about them. But Mr. Ophir, a student-turned-researcher, thought multitaskers might be rewiring themselves to handle the load.

His passion was personal. He had spent seven years in Israeli intelligence after being weeded out of the air force — partly, he felt, because he was not a good multitasker. Could his brain be retrained?

Mr. Ophir, like others around the country studying how technology bent the brain, was startled by what he discovered.

THE MYTH OF MULTITASKING

The test subjects were divided into two groups: those classified as heavy multitaskers based on their answers to questions about how they used technology, and those who were not.

In a test created by Mr. Ophir and his colleagues, subjects at a computer were briefly shown an image of red rectangles. Then they saw a similar image and were asked whether any of the rectangles had moved. It was a simple task until the addition of a twist: blue rectangles were added, and the subjects were told to ignore them.

The multitaskers then did a significantly worse job than the non-multitaskers at recognizing whether red rectangles had changed position. In other words, they had trouble filtering out the blue ones — the irrelevant information.

So, too, the multitaskers took longer than non-multitaskers to switch among tasks, like differentiating vowels from consonants and then odd from even numbers. The multitaskers were shown to be less efficient at juggling problems.

Other tests at Stanford, an important center for research in this fast-growing field, showed multitaskers tended to search for new information rather than accept a reward for putting older, more valuable information to work.

Researchers say these findings point to an interesting dynamic: multitaskers seem more sensitive than non-multitaskers to incoming information.

The results also illustrate an age-old conflict in the brain, one that technology may be intensifying. A portion of the brain acts as a control tower, helping a person focus and set priorities. More primitive parts of the brain, like those that process sight and sound, demand that it pay attention to new information, bombarding the control tower when they are stimulated.

Researchers say there is an evolutionary rationale for the pressure this barrage puts on the brain. The lower-brain functions alert humans to danger, like a nearby lion, overriding goals like building a hut. In the modern world, the chime of incoming e-mail can override the goal of writing a business plan or playing catch with the children.

"Throughout evolutionary history, a big surprise would get everyone's brain thinking," said Clifford Nass, a communications professor at Stanford. "But we've got a large and growing group of people who think the slightest hint that something interesting might be going on is like catnip. They can't ignore it."

Mr. Nass says the Stanford studies are important because they show multitasking's lingering effects: "The scary part for guys like Kord is, they can't shut off their multitasking tendencies when they're not multitasking."

Melina Uncapher, a neurobiologist on the Stanford team, said she and other researchers were unsure whether the muddied multitaskers were simply prone to distraction and would have had trouble focusing in any era. But she added that the idea that information overload causes distraction was supported by more and more research.

A study at the University of California, Irvine, found that people interrupted by e-mail reported significantly increased stress compared with those left to focus. Stress hormones have been shown to reduce short-term memory, said Gary Small, a psychiatrist at the University of California, Los Angeles.

Preliminary research shows some people can more easily juggle multiple information streams. These "supertaskers" represent less than 3 percent of the population, according to scientists at the University of Utah.

Other research shows computer use has neurological advantages. In imaging studies, Dr. Small observed that Internet users showed greater brain activity than nonusers, suggesting they were growing their neural circuitry.

At the University of Rochester, researchers found that players of some fast-paced video games can track the movement of a third more objects on a screen than nonplayers. They say the games can improve reaction and the ability to pick out details amid clutter.

"In a sense, those games have a very strong both rehabilitative and educational power," said the lead researcher, Daphne Bavelier, who is working with others in the field to channel these changes into real-world benefits like safer driving.

There is a vibrant debate among scientists over whether technology's influence on behavior and the brain is good or bad, and how significant it is.

"The bottom line is, the brain is wired to adapt," said Steven Yantis, a professor of brain sciences at Johns Hopkins University. "There's no question that rewiring goes on all the time," he added. But he said it was too early to say whether the changes caused by technology were materially different from others in the past.

Mr. Ophir is loath to call the cognitive changes bad or good, though the impact on analysis and creativity worries him.

He is not just worried about other people. Shortly after he came to Stanford, a professor thanked him for being the one student in class paying full attention and not using a computer or phone. But he recently began using an iPhone and noticed a change; he felt its pull, even when playing with his daughter.

"The media is changing me," he said. "I hear this internal ping that says: check e-mail and voice mail."

"I have to work to suppress it."

Kord Campbell does not bother to suppress it, or no longer can.

INTERRUPTED BY A CORPSE

It is a Wednesday in April, and in 10 minutes, Mr. Campbell has an online conference call that could determine the fate of his new venture, called Loggly. It makes software that helps companies understand the clicking and buying patterns of their online customers.

Mr. Campbell and his colleagues, each working from a home office, are frantically trying to set up a program that will let them share images with executives at their prospective partner.

But at the moment when Mr. Campbell most needs to focus on that urgent task, something else competes for his attention: "Man Found Dead Inside His Business."

That is the tweet that appears on the left-most of Mr. Campbell's array of monitors, which he has expanded to three screens, at times adding a laptop and an iPad.

On the left screen, Mr. Campbell follows the tweets of 1,100 people, along with instant messages and group chats. The middle monitor displays a dark field filled with computer code, along with Skype, a service that allows Mr. Campbell to talk to his colleagues, sometimes using video. The monitor on the right keeps e-mail, a calendar, a Web browser and a music player.

Even with the meeting fast approaching, Mr. Campbell cannot resist the tweet about the corpse. He clicks on the link in it, glances at the article and dismisses it. "It's some article about something somewhere," he says, annoyed by the ads for jeans popping up.

The program gets fixed, and the meeting turns out to be fruitful: the partners are ready to do business. A colleague says via instant message: "YES."

Other times, Mr. Campbell's information juggling has taken a more serious toll. A few weeks earlier, he once again overlooked an e-mail message from a prospective investor. Another time, Mr. Campbell signed the company up for the wrong type of business account on Amazon.com, costing $300 a month for six months before he got around to correcting it. He has burned hamburgers on the grill, forgotten to pick up the children and lingered in the bathroom playing video games on an iPhone.

Mr. Campbell can be unaware of his own habits. In a two-and-a-half hour stretch one recent morning, he switched rapidly between e-mail and several other programs, according to data from RescueTime, which monitored his computer use with his permission. But when asked later what he was doing in that period, Mr. Campbell said he had been on a long Skype call, and "may have pulled up an e-mail or two."

The kind of disconnection Mr. Campbell experiences is not an entirely new problem, of course. As they did in earlier eras, people can become so lost in work, hobbies or TV that they fail to pay attention to family.

Mr. Campbell concedes that, even without technology, he may work or play obsessively, just as his father immersed himself in crossword puzzles. But he says this era is different because he can multitask anyplace, anytime.

"It's a mixed blessing," he said. "If you're not careful, your marriage can fall apart or your kids can be ready to play and you'll get distracted."

THE TOLL ON CHILDREN

Father and son sit in armchairs. Controllers in hand, they engage in a fierce video game battle, displayed on the nearby flat-panel TV, as Lily watches.

They are playing Super Smash Bros. Brawl, a cartoonish animated fight between characters that battle using anvils, explosives and other weapons.

“Kill him, Dad,” Lily screams. To no avail. Connor regularly beats his father, prompting expletives and, once, a thrown pillow. But there is bonding and mutual respect.

“He’s a lot more tactical,” says Connor. “But I’m really good at quick reflexes.”

Screens big and small are central to the Campbell family’s leisure time. Connor and his mother relax while watching TV shows like “Heroes.” Lily has an iPod Touch, a portable DVD player and her own laptop, which she uses to watch videos, listen to music and play games.

Lily, a second-grader, is allowed only an hour a day of unstructured time, which she often spends with her devices. The laptop can consume her.

“When she’s on it, you can holler her name all day and she won’t hear,” Mrs. Campbell said.

Researchers worry that constant digital stimulation like this creates attention problems for children with brains that are still developing, who already struggle to set priorities and resist impulses.

Connor’s troubles started late last year. He could not focus on homework. No wonder, perhaps. On his bedroom desk sit two monitors, one with his music collection, one with Facebook and Reddit, a social site with news links that he and his father love. His iPhone availed him to relentless texting with his girlfriend.

When he studied, “a little voice would be saying, ‘Look up’ at the computer, and I’d look up,” Connor said. “Normally, I’d say I want to only read for a few minutes, but I’d search every corner of Reddit and then check Facebook.”

His Web browsing informs him. “He’s a fact hound,” Mr. Campbell brags. “Connor is, other than programming, extremely technical. He’s 100 percent Internet savvy.”

But the parents worry too. “Connor is obsessed,” his mother said. “Kord says we have to teach him balance.”

So in January, they held a family meeting. Study time now takes place in a group setting at the dinner table after everyone has finished eating. It feels, Mr. Campbell says, like togetherness.

NO VACATIONS

For spring break, the family rented a cottage in Carmel, Calif. Mrs. Campbell hoped everyone would unplug.

But the day before they left, the iPad from Apple came out, and Mr. Campbell snapped one up. The next night, their first on vacation, "We didn't go out to dinner," Mrs. Campbell mourned. "We just sat there on our devices."

She rallied the troops the next day to the aquarium. Her husband joined them for a bit but then begged out to do e-mail on his phone.

Later she found him playing video games.

The trip came as Mr. Campbell was trying to raise several million dollars for his new venture, a goal that he achieved. Brenda said she understood that his pursuit required intensity but was less understanding of the accompanying surge in video game.

His behavior brought about a discussion between them. Mrs. Campbell said he told her that he was capable of logging off, citing a trip to Hawaii several years ago that they called their second honeymoon.

"What trip are you thinking about?" she said she asked him. She recalled that he had spent two hours a day online in the hotel's business center.

On Thursday, their fourth day in Carmel, Mr. Campbell spent the day at the beach with his family. They flew a kite and played whiffle ball.

Connor unplugged too. "It changes the mood of everything when everybody is present," Mrs. Campbell said.

The next day, the family drove home, and Mr. Campbell disappeared into his office.

Technology use is growing for Mrs. Campbell as well. She divides her time between keeping the books of her husband's company, home-making and working at the school library. She checks e-mail 25 times a day, sends texts and uses Facebook.

Recently, she was baking peanut butter cookies for Teacher Appreciation Day when her phone chimed in the living room. She answered a text, then became lost in Facebook, forgot about the cookies and burned them. She started a new batch, but heard the phone again, got lost in messaging, and burned those too. Out of ingredients and shamed, she bought cookies at the store.

She feels less focused and has trouble completing projects. Some days, she promises herself she will ignore her device. "It's like a diet — you have good intentions in the morning and then you're like, 'There went that,' " she said.

Mr. Nass at Stanford thinks the ultimate risk of heavy technology use is that it diminishes empathy by limiting how much people engage with one another, even in the same room.

"The way we become more human is by paying attention to each other," he said. "It shows how much you care."

That empathy, Mr. Nass said, is essential to the human condition. "We are at an inflection point," he said. "A significant fraction of people's experiences are now fragmented."

An Ugly Toll of Technology: Impatience and Forgetfulness

BY TARA PARKER-POPE | JUNE 6, 2010

ARE YOUR FACEBOOK FRIENDS more interesting than those you have in real life?

Has high-speed Internet made you impatient with slow-speed children?

Do you sometimes think about reaching for the fast-forward button, only to realize that life does not come with a remote control?

If you answered yes to any of those questions, exposure to technology may be slowly reshaping your personality. Some experts believe excessive use of the Internet, cellphones and other technologies can cause us to become more impatient, impulsive, forgetful and even more narcissistic.

"More and more, life is resembling the chat room," says Dr. Elias Aboujaoude, director of the Impulse Control Disorders Clinic at Stanford. "We're paying a price in terms of our cognitive life because of this virtual lifestyle."

We do spend a lot of time with our devices, and some studies have suggested that excessive dependence on cellphones and the Internet is akin to an addiction. Web sites like NetAddiction.com offer self-assessment tests to determine if technology has become a drug. Among the questions used to identify those at risk: Do you neglect housework to spend more time online? Are you frequently checking your e-mail? Do you often lose sleep because you log in late at night? If you answered "often" or "always," technology may be taking a toll on you.

In a study to be published in the journal Cyberpsychology, Behavior and Social Networking, researchers from the University of Melbourne in Australia subjected 173 college students to tests measuring risk for problematic Internet and gambling behaviors. About 5 percent of the students showed signs of gambling problems, but 10 percent of the students posted scores high enough to put them in the at-risk category for Internet "addiction."

Technology use was clearly interfering with the students' daily lives, but it may be going too far to call it an addiction, says Nicki Dowling, a clinical psychologist who led the study. Ms. Dowling prefers to call it "Internet dependence."

Typically, the concern about our dependence on technology is that it detracts from our time with family and friends in the real world. But psychologists have become intrigued by a more subtle and insidious effect of our online interactions. It may be that the immediacy of the Internet, the efficiency of the iPhone and the anonymity of the chat room change the core of who we are, issues that Dr. Aboujaoude explores in a book, "Virtually You: The Internet and the Fracturing of the Self," to be released next year.

Dr. Aboujaoude also asks whether the vast storage available in e-mail and on the Internet is preventing many of us from letting go, causing us to retain many old and unnecessary memories at the expense of making new ones. Everything is saved these days, he notes, from the meaningless e-mail sent after a work lunch to the angry online exchange with a spouse.

"If you can't forget because all this stuff is staring at you, what does that do to your ability to lay down new memories and remember things that you should be remembering?" Dr. Aboujaoude said. "When you have 500 pictures from your vacation in your Flickr account, as opposed to five pictures that are really meaningful, does that change your ability to recall the moments that you really want to recall?"

There is also no easy way to conquer a dependence on technology. Nicholas Carr, author of the new book "The Shallows: What the Internet Is Doing to Our Brains," says that social and family responsibilities, work and other pressures influence our use of technology. "The deeper a technology is woven into the patterns of everyday life, the less choice we have about whether and how we use that technology," Mr. Carr wrote in a recent blog post on the topic.

Some experts suggest simply trying to curtail the amount of time you spend online. Set limits for how often you check e-mail or force yourself to leave your cellphone at home occasionally.

The problem is similar to an eating disorder, says Dr. Kimberly Young, a professor at St. Bonaventure University in New York who has led research on the addictive nature of online technology. Technology, like food, is an essential part of daily life, and those suffering from disordered online behavior cannot give it up entirely and instead have to learn moderation and controlled use. She suggests therapy to determine the underlying issues that set off a person's need to use the Internet "as a way of escape."

The International Center for Media and the Public Agenda at the University of Maryland asked 200 students to refrain from using electronic media for a day. The reports from students after the study suggest that giving up technology cold turkey not only makes life logistically difficult, but also changes our ability to connect with others.

"Texting and I.M.'ing my friends gives me a constant feeling of comfort," wrote one student. "When I did not have those two luxuries, I felt quite alone and secluded from my life. Although I go to a school with thousands of students, the fact that I was not able to communicate with anyone via technology was almost unbearable."

Growing Up Digital, Wired for Distraction

BY MATT RICHTEL | NOV. 21, 2010

REDWOOD CITY, CALIF. — On the eve of a pivotal academic year in Vishal Singh's life, he faces a stark choice on his bedroom desk: book or computer?

By all rights, Vishal, a bright 17-year-old, should already have finished the book, Kurt Vonnegut's "Cat's Cradle," his summer reading assignment. But he has managed 43 pages in two months.

He typically favors Facebook, YouTube and making digital videos. That is the case this August afternoon. Bypassing Vonnegut, he clicks over to YouTube, meaning that tomorrow he will enter his senior year of high school hoping to see an improvement in his grades, but without having completed his only summer homework.

On YouTube, "you can get a whole story in six minutes," he explains. "A book takes so long. I prefer the immediate gratification."

Students have always faced distractions and time-wasters. But computers and cellphones, and the constant stream of stimuli they offer, pose a profound new challenge to focusing and learning.

Researchers say the lure of these technologies, while it affects adults too, is particularly powerful for young people. The risk, they say, is that developing brains can become more easily habituated than adult brains to constantly switching tasks — and less able to sustain attention.

"Their brains are rewarded not for staying on task but for jumping to the next thing," said Michael Rich, an associate professor at Harvard Medical School and executive director of the Center on Media and Child Health in Boston. And the effects could linger: "The worry is we're raising a generation of kids in front of screens whose brains are going to be wired differently."

But even as some parents and educators express unease about students' digital diets, they are intensifying efforts to use technology in the classroom, seeing it as a way to connect with students and give them essential skills. Across the country, schools are equipping themselves with computers, Internet access and mobile devices so they can teach on the students' technological territory.

It is a tension on vivid display at Vishal's school, Woodside High School, on a sprawling campus set against the forested hills of Silicon Valley. Here, as elsewhere, it is not uncommon for students to send hundreds of text messages a day or spend hours playing video games, and virtually everyone is on Facebook.

The principal, David Reilly, 37, a former musician who says he sympathizes when young people feel disenfranchised, is determined to engage these 21st-century students. He has asked teachers to build Web sites to communicate with students, introduced popular classes on using digital tools to record music, secured funding for iPads to teach Mandarin and obtained $3 million in grants for a multimedia center.

He pushed first period back an hour, to 9 a.m., because students were showing up bleary-eyed, at least in part because they were up late on their computers. Unchecked use of digital devices, he says, can create a culture in which students are addicted to the virtual world and lost in it.

"I am trying to take back their attention from their BlackBerrys and video games," he says. "To a degree, I'm using technology to do it."

The same tension surfaces in Vishal, whose ability to be distracted by computers is rivaled by his proficiency with them. At the beginning of his junior year, he discovered a passion for filmmaking and made a name for himself among friends and teachers with his storytelling in videos made with digital cameras and editing software.

He acts as his family's tech-support expert, helping his father, Satendra, a lab manager, retrieve lost documents on the computer, and his mother, Indra, a security manager at the San Francisco airport, build her own Web site.

But he also plays video games 10 hours a week. He regularly sends

JIM WILSON/THE NEW YORK TIMES

Students at Woodside High School are often reminded of the restrictions on their phones at school.

Facebook status updates at 2 a.m., even on school nights, and has such a reputation for distributing links to videos that his best friend calls him a "YouTube bully."

Several teachers call Vishal one of their brightest students, and they wonder why things are not adding up. Last semester, his grade point average was 2.3 after a D-plus in English and an F in Algebra II. He got an A in film critique.

"He's a kid caught between two worlds," said Mr. Reilly — one that is virtual and one with real-life demands.

Vishal, like his mother, says he lacks the self-control to favor schoolwork over the computer. She sat him down a few weeks before school started and told him that, while she respected his passion for film and his technical skills, he had to use them productively.

"This is the year," she says she told him. "This is your senior year and you can't afford not to focus."

JIM WILSON/THE NEW YORK TIMES

Vishal Singh, 17, often chooses time on his computer over doing homework. Vishal, whose lighting gear is on the bed, is an aspiring filmmaker.

It was not always this way. As a child, Vishal had a tendency to procrastinate, but nothing like this. Something changed him.

GROWING UP WITH GADGETS

When he was 3, Vishal moved with his parents and older brother to their current home, a three-bedroom house in the working-class section of Redwood City, a suburb in Silicon Valley that is more diverse than some of its elite neighbors.

Thin and quiet with a shy smile, Vishal passed the admissions test for a prestigious public elementary and middle school. Until sixth grade, he focused on homework, regularly going to the house of a good friend to study with him.

But Vishal and his family say two things changed around the seventh grade: his mother went back to work, and he got a computer. He became increasingly engrossed in games and surfing the Internet, finding an easy outlet for what he describes as an inclination to procrastinate.

"I realized there were choices," Vishal recalls. "Homework wasn't the only option."

Several recent studies show that young people tend to use home computers for entertainment, not learning, and that this can hurt school performance, particularly in low-income families. Jacob L. Vigdor, an economics professor at Duke University who led some of the research, said that when adults were not supervising computer use, children "are left to their own devices, and the impetus isn't to do homework but play around."

Research also shows that students often juggle homework and entertainment. The Kaiser Family Foundation found earlier this year that half of students from 8 to 18 are using the Internet, watching TV or using some other form of media either "most" (31 percent) or "some" (25 percent) of the time that they are doing homework.

At Woodside, as elsewhere, students' use of technology is not uniform. Mr. Reilly, the principal, says their choices tend to reflect their personalities. Social butterflies tend to be heavy texters and Facebook users. Students who are less social might escape into games, while drifters or those prone to procrastination, like Vishal, might surf the Web or watch videos.

The technology has created on campuses a new set of social types — not the thespian and the jock but the texter and gamer, Facebook addict and YouTube potato.

"The technology amplifies whoever you are," Mr. Reilly says.

For some, the amplification is intense. Allison Miller, 14, sends and receives 27,000 texts in a month, her fingers clicking at a blistering pace as she carries on as many as seven text conversations at a time. She texts between classes, at the moment soccer practice ends, while being driven to and from school and, often, while studying.

Most of the exchanges are little more than quick greetings, but they can get more in-depth, like "if someone tells you about a drama going on with someone," Allison said. "I can text one person while talking on the phone to someone else."

But this proficiency comes at a cost: she blames multitasking for the three B's on her recent progress report.

"I'll be reading a book for homework and I'll get a text message and pause my reading and put down the book, pick up the phone to reply to the text message, and then 20 minutes later realize, 'Oh, I forgot to do my homework.' "

Some shyer students do not socialize through technology — they recede into it. Ramon Ochoa-Lopez, 14, an introvert, plays six hours of video games on weekdays and more on weekends, leaving homework to be done in the bathroom before school.

Escaping into games can also salve teenagers' age-old desire for some control in their chaotic lives. "It's a way for me to separate myself," Ramon says. "If there's an argument between my mom and one of my brothers, I'll just go to my room and start playing video games and escape."

With powerful new cellphones, the interactive experience can go everywhere. Between classes at Woodside or at lunch, when use of personal devices is permitted, students gather in clusters, sometimes chatting face to face, sometimes half-involved in a conversation while texting someone across the teeming quad. Others sit alone, watching a video, listening to music or updating Facebook.

Students say that their parents, worried about the distractions, try to police computer time, but that monitoring the use of cellphones is difficult. Parents may also want to be able to call their children at any time, so taking the phone away is not always an option.

Other parents wholly embrace computer use, even when it has no obvious educational benefit.

"If you're not on top of technology, you're not going to be on top of the world," said John McMullen, 56, a retired criminal investigator whose son, Sean, is one of five friends in the group Vishal joins for lunch each day.

Sean's favorite medium is video games; he plays for four hours after school and twice that on weekends. He was playing more but found his habit pulling his grade point average below 3.2, the point at which he felt comfortable. He says he sometimes wishes that his parents would force him to quit playing and study, because he finds it hard to quit when given the choice. Still, he says, video games are not responsible for his lack of focus, asserting that in another era he would have been distracted by TV or something else.

"Video games don't make the hole; they fill it," says Sean, sitting at a picnic table in the quad, where he is surrounded by a multimillion-dollar view: on the nearby hills are the evergreens that tower above the affluent neighborhoods populated by Internet tycoons. Sean, a senior, concedes that video games take a physical toll: "I haven't done exercise since my sophomore year. But that doesn't seem like a big deal. I still look the same."

Sam Crocker, Vishal's closest friend, who has straight A's but lower SAT scores than he would like, blames the Internet's distractions for his inability to finish either of his two summer reading books.

"I know I can read a book, but then I'm up and checking Facebook," he says, adding: "Facebook is amazing because it feels like you're doing something and you're not doing anything. It's the absence of doing something, but you feel gratified anyway."

He concludes: "My attention span is getting worse."

THE LURE OF DISTRACTION

Some neuroscientists have been studying people like Sam and Vishal. They have begun to understand what happens to the brains of young people who are constantly online and in touch.

In an experiment at the German Sport University in Cologne in 2007, boys from 12 to 14 spent an hour each night playing video games after they finished homework.

On alternate nights, the boys spent an hour watching an exciting movie, like "Harry Potter" or "Star Trek," rather than playing video games. That allowed the researchers to compare the effect of video games and TV.

The researchers looked at how the use of these media affected the boys' brainwave patterns while sleeping and their ability to remember their homework in the subsequent days. They found that playing video games led to markedly lower sleep quality than watching TV, and also led to a "significant decline" in the boys' ability to remember vocabulary words. The findings were published in the journal Pediatrics.

Markus Dworak, a researcher who led the study and is now a neuroscientist at Harvard, said it was not clear whether the boys' learning suffered because sleep was disrupted or, as he speculates, also because the intensity of the game experience overrode the brain's recording of the vocabulary.

"When you look at vocabulary and look at huge stimulus after that, your brain has to decide which information to store," he said. "Your brain might favor the emotionally stimulating information over the vocabulary."

At the University of California, San Francisco, scientists have found that when rats have a new experience, like exploring an unfamiliar area, their brains show new patterns of activity. But only when the rats take a break from their exploration do they process those patterns in a way that seems to create a persistent memory.

In that vein, recent imaging studies of people have found that major cross sections of the brain become surprisingly active during downtime. These brain studies suggest to researchers that periods of rest are critical in allowing the brain to synthesize information, make connections between ideas and even develop the sense of self.

Researchers say these studies have particular implications for young people, whose brains have more trouble focusing and setting priorities.

"Downtime is to the brain what sleep is to the body," said Dr. Rich of Harvard Medical School. "But kids are in a constant mode of stimulation."

“The headline is: bring back boredom,” added Dr. Rich, who last month gave a speech to the American Academy of Pediatrics entitled, “Finding Huck Finn: Reclaiming Childhood from the River of Electronic Screens.”

Dr. Rich said in an interview that he was not suggesting young people should toss out their devices, but rather that they embrace a more balanced approach to what he said were powerful tools necessary to compete and succeed in modern life.

The heavy use of devices also worries Daniel Anderson, a professor of psychology at the University of Massachusetts at Amherst, who is known for research showing that children are not as harmed by TV viewing as some researchers have suggested.

Multitasking using ubiquitous, interactive and highly stimulating computers and phones, Professor Anderson says, appears to have a more powerful effect than TV.

Like Dr. Rich, he says he believes that young, developing brains are becoming habituated to distraction and to switching tasks, not to focus.

“If you’ve grown up processing multiple media, that’s exactly the mode you’re going to fall into when put in that environment — you develop a need for that stimulation,” he said.

Vishal can attest to that.

“I’m doing Facebook, YouTube, having a conversation or two with a friend, listening to music at the same time. I’m doing a million things at once, like a lot of people my age,” he says. “Sometimes I’ll say: I need to stop this and do my schoolwork, but I can’t.”

“If it weren’t for the Internet, I’d focus more on school and be doing better academically,” he says. But thanks to the Internet, he says, he has discovered and pursued his passion: filmmaking. Without the Internet, “I also wouldn’t know what I want to do with my life.”

CLICKING TOWARD A FUTURE

The woman sits in a cemetery at dusk, sobbing. Behind her, silhouetted and translucent, a man kneels, then fades away, a ghost.

This captivating image appears on Vishal's computer screen. On this Thursday afternoon in late September, he is engrossed in scenes he shot the previous weekend for a music video he is making with his cousin.

The video is based on a song performed by the band Guns N' Roses about a woman whose boyfriend dies. He wants it to be part of the package of work he submits to colleges that emphasize film study, along with a documentary he is making about home-schooled students.

Now comes the editing. Vishal taught himself to use sophisticated editing software in part by watching tutorials on YouTube. He does not leave his chair for more than two hours, sipping Pepsi, his face often inches from the screen, as he perfects the clip from the cemetery. The image of the crying woman was shot separately from the image of the kneeling man, and he is trying to fuse them.

"I'm spending two hours to get a few seconds just right," he says.

He occasionally sends a text message or checks Facebook, but he is focused in a way he rarely is when doing homework. He says the chief difference is that filmmaking feels applicable to his chosen future, and he hopes colleges, like the University of Southern California or the California Institute of the Arts in Los Angeles, will be so impressed by his portfolio that they will overlook his school performance.

"This is going to compensate for the grades," he says. On this day, his homework includes a worksheet for Latin, some reading for English class and an economics essay, but they can wait.

For Vishal, there's another clear difference between filmmaking and homework: interactivity. As he edits, the windows on the screen come alive; every few seconds, he clicks the mouse to make tiny changes to the lighting and flow of the images, and the software gives him constant feedback.

"I click and something happens," he says, explaining that, by comparison, reading a book or doing homework is less exciting. "I guess it goes back to the immediate gratification thing."

The $2,000 computer Vishal is using is state of the art and only a week old. It represents a concession by his parents. They allowed him to buy it, despite their continuing concerns about his technology habits, because they wanted to support his filmmaking dream. "If we put roadblocks in his way, he's just going to get depressed," his mother says. Besides, she adds, "he's been making an effort to do his homework."

At this point in the semester, it seems she is right. The first schoolwide progress reports come out in late September, and Vishal has mostly A's and B's. He says he has been able to make headway by applying himself, but also by cutting back his workload. Unlike last year, he is not taking advanced placement classes, and he has chosen to retake Algebra II not in the classroom but in an online class that lets him work at his own pace.

His shift to easier classes might not please college admissions officers, according to Woodside's college adviser, Zorina Matavulj. She says they want seniors to intensify their efforts. As it is, she says, even if Vishal improves his performance significantly, someone with his grades faces long odds in applying to the kinds of colleges he aspires to.

Still, Vishal's passion for film reinforces for Mr. Reilly, the principal, that the way to reach these students is on their own terms.

HANDS-ON TECHNOLOGY

Big Macintosh monitors sit on every desk, and a man with hip glasses and an easygoing style stands at the front of the class. He is Geoff Diesel, 40, a favorite teacher here at Woodside who has taught English and film. Now he teaches one of Mr. Reilly's new classes, audio production. He has a rapt audience of more than 20 students as he shows a video of the band Nirvana mixing their music, then holds up a music keyboard.

"Who knows how to use Pro Tools? We've got it. It's the program used by the best music studios in the world," he says.

In the back of the room, Mr. Reilly watches, thrilled. He introduced the audio course last year and enough students signed up to fill four classes. (He could barely pull together one class when he introduced Mandarin, even though he had secured iPads to help teach the language.)

"Some of these students are our most at-risk kids," he says. He means that they are more likely to tune out school, skip class or not do their homework, and that they may not get healthful meals at home. They may also do their most enthusiastic writing not for class but in text messages and on Facebook. "They're here, they're in class, they're listening."

Despite Woodside High's affluent setting, about 40 percent of its 1,800 students come from low-income families and receive a reduced-cost or free lunch. The school is 56 percent Latino, 38 percent white and 5 percent African-American, and it sends 93 percent of its students to four-year or community colleges.

Mr. Reilly says that the audio class provides solid vocational training and can get students interested in other subjects.

"Today mixing music, tomorrow sound waves and physics," he says. And he thinks the key is that they love not just the music but getting their hands on the technology. "We're meeting them on their turf."

It does not mean he sees technology as a panacea. "I'll always take one great teacher in a cave over a dozen Smart Boards," he says, referring to the high-tech teaching displays used in many schools.

Teachers at Woodside commonly blame technology for students' struggles to concentrate, but they are divided over whether embracing computers is the right solution.

"It's a catastrophe," said Alan Eaton, a charismatic Latin teacher. He says that technology has led to a "balkanization of their focus and duration of stamina," and that schools make the problem worse when they adopt the technology.

"When rock 'n' roll came about, we didn't start using it in classrooms like we're doing with technology," he says. He personally feels the sting, since his advanced classes have one-third as many students as they had a decade ago.

Vishal remains a Latin student, one whom Mr. Eaton describes as particularly bright. But the teacher wonders if technology might be the reason Vishal seems to lose interest in academics the minute he leaves class.

Mr. Diesel, by contrast, does not think technology is behind the problems of Vishal and his schoolmates — in fact, he thinks it is the key to connecting with them, and an essential tool. "It's in their DNA to look at screens," he asserts. And he offers another analogy to explain his approach: "Frankenstein is in the room and I don't want him to tear me apart. If I'm not using technology, I lose them completely."

Mr. Diesel had Vishal as a student in cinema class and describes him as a "breath of fresh air" with a gift for filmmaking. Mr. Diesel says he wonders if Vishal is a bit like Woody Allen, talented but not interested in being part of the system.

But Mr. Diesel adds: "If Vishal's going to be an independent filmmaker, he's got to read Vonnegut. If you're going to write scripts, you've got to read."

BACK TO READING ALOUD

Vishal sits near the back of English IV. Marcia Blondel, a veteran teacher, asks the students to open the book they are studying, "The Things They Carried," which is about the Vietnam War.

"Who wants to read starting in the middle of Page 137?" she asks. One student begins to read aloud, and the rest follow along.

To Ms. Blondel, the exercise in group reading represents a regression in American education and an indictment of technology. The reason she has to do it, she says, is that students now lack the attention span to read the assignments on their own.

"How can you have a discussion in class?" she complains, arguing that she has seen a considerable change in recent years. In some classes she can count on little more than one-third of the students to read a 30-page homework assignment.

She adds: "You can't become a good writer by watching YouTube, texting and e-mailing a bunch of abbreviations."

As the group-reading effort winds down, she says gently: "I hope this will motivate you to read on your own."

It is a reminder of the choices that have followed the students through the semester: computer or homework? Immediate gratification or investing in the future?

Mr. Reilly hopes that the two can meet — that computers can be combined with education to better engage students and can give them technical skills without compromising deep analytical thought.

But in Vishal's case, computers and schoolwork seem more and more to be mutually exclusive. Ms. Blondel says that Vishal, after a decent start to the school year, has fallen into bad habits. In October, he turned in weeks late, for example, a short essay based on the first few chapters of "The Things They Carried." His grade at that point, she says, tracks around a D.

For his part, Vishal says he is investing himself more in his filmmaking, accelerating work with his cousin on their music video project. But he is also using Facebook late at night and surfing for videos on YouTube. The evidence of the shift comes in a string of Facebook updates.

Saturday, 11:55 p.m.: "Editing, editing, editing"

Sunday, 3:55 p.m.: "8+ hours of shooting, 8+ hours of editing. All for just a three-minute scene. Mind = Dead."

Sunday, 11:00 p.m.: "Fun day, finally got to spend a day relaxing... now about that homework..."

MALIA WOLLAN contributed reporting.

When You Text Till You Drop

REVIEW | BY BRYAN BURROUGH | MAY 12, 2012

I DON'T KNOW about you, but I've always found the debate about what our mobile devices are doing to us — to our behaviors, our manners, our minds — at least as interesting as reports about what we're doing with these devices.

What about that gent who was talking loudly into his Android phone on the Metro-North train this morning? Was he really that obnoxious before we all went wireless — or did the device somehow change him? And what about all those young people who spend hours upon hours texting and sexting and Facebooking? What kinds of adults will they become?

Is the casual anonymity of Internet discussion turning us into boors? What did we once do with all the hours we now spend obsessively checking e-mail and texts? Smoke?

Larry D. Rosen, a California psychologist, is less concerned with techno-boorishness than with the very real possibility that all these new personal gadgets may be making some of us mentally ill — especially those who are prone to narcissism, for example, or to depression or obsessive-compulsive disorder.

In "iDisorder: Understanding Our Obsession With Technology and Overcoming Its Hold on Us" (Palgrave Macmillan), Dr. Rosen surveys the existing research, throws in a bit of his own and suggests ways that users of new technologies can avoid behavioral pitfalls.

As much as the topic interests me, I was initially skeptical of this book. For one thing, it's a little proud of itself. The word "iDisorder," which Dr. Rosen repeats throughout, suggests an author trying very hard to coin a term. He is among the few authors I've seen who refers to his own book as "groundbreaking."

Yet "iDisorder" is a pleasant surprise — lean, thoughtful, clearly written and full of ideas and data you'll want to throw into dinner-party conversation. Did you know that psychologists divide Twitter users into "informers," those who pass along interesting facts, and "meformers," those who pass along interesting facts about only themselves? Or that 70 percent of those who report heavily using mobile devices experience "phantom vibration syndrome," which is what happens when your pocket buzzes and there's no phone in your pocket? (I thought I was the only one.) Or that heavy use of Facebook has been linked to mood swings among some teenagers? Researchers are calling this "Facebook depression." (And I thought that my children were just having a lot of bad days.)

One strength of "iDisorder" is Dr. Rosen's cleareyed view of technology and its uses. He doesn't oppose it. In fact, his view is quite the opposite. What we need, he says, is a sense of restorative balance and self-awareness. It is unavoidable that many of us will fall prey to an iDisorder, he says, but "it is not fatal and we are not doomed to spend time in a mental institution or a rehab center." By using a few simple strategies, he says, "we can safely emerge from our TechnoCocoons and rejoin the world of the healthy."

The book's chapters focus on mental health challenges linked to heavy technology use. They include how social media sites may spawn narcissism (no surprise there) and how constantly checking our wireless mobile devices (he calls them W.M.D.'s, a great acronym) can lead to obsessive-compulsive disorder. Others look at how technology addiction can lead to attention-deficit hyperactivity disorder, and at how all that medical data available online has created a class of people known as "cyberchondriacs." Perhaps most interesting of all, Dr. Rosen examines how the constant use of technology may be rewiring our brains. One study he cites calls the impact on memory the "Google effect," that is, an inability to remember facts brought on by the realization that they are all available in a few keystrokes via Google.

At the end of each chapter, Dr. Rosen details a list of things that can be done to combat each techno-disorder. These tend to be a bit repetitive and common-sensical, but that doesn't make them any less useful. One often-suggested solution is to take a "tech break." In other words, if overusing your iPad is making you crazy, maybe you should stop using it so much. I know: duh. But still.

For those combating some form of techno-addiction, Dr. Rosen advises regularly stepping away from the computer for a few minutes and connecting with nature; just standing in your driveway and staring at the bushes, research shows, has a way of resetting our brains.

Parents will find this book particularly helpful. Dr. Rosen suggests a whole set of remedies for children's techno-addiction. Two popular methods are to make sure your child gets a full night's sleep, and to convene regular family dinners where technology is forbidden at the table. This is especially useful, it appears, in reintroducing children to normal interaction after hours spent in cyberconversation.

For those worried about their own heavy use of technology, or their family's, this book could be a helpful starting point for understanding the consequences, and for overcoming them.

Disruptions: More Connected, Yet More Alone

BY NICK BILTON | SEPT. 1, 2013

SAN FRANCISCO — Last weekend, I was watching television with a few friends, browsing the week's most popular YouTube videos, when a piece in the comedy section called "I Forgot My Phone" caught my eye. As I was about to click play, however, a friend warned, "Oh, don't watch that. I saw it yesterday, and it's really sad."

The two-minute video, which has been viewed more than 15 million times, begins with a couple in bed. The woman, played by the comedian and actress Charlene deGuzman, stares silently while her boyfriend pays no mind and checks his smartphone.

The subsequent scenes follow Ms. deGuzman through a day that is downright dystopian: people ignore her as they stare at their phones during lunch, at a concert, while bowling and at a birthday party. (Even the birthday boy is recording the party on his phone.) The clip ends with Ms. deGuzman back in bed with her boyfriend at the end of the day; he is still using his phone.

Ms. deGuzman's video makes for some discomfiting viewing. It's a direct hit on our smartphone-obsessed culture, needling us about our addiction to that little screen and suggesting that maybe life is just better led when it is lived rather than viewed. While the clip has funny scenes — a man proposing on a beach while trying to record the special moment on his phone — it is mostly ... sad.

"I came up with the idea for the video when I started to realize how ridiculous we are all being, myself included, when I was at a concert and people around me were recording the show with their phones, not actually watching the concert," Ms. deGuzman said in an interview.

"It makes me sad that there are moments in our lives where we're not present because we're looking at a phone," said Ms. deGuzman, who also wrote the piece, which was directed by Miles Crawford. She mused that, like it or not, experiencing life through a four-inch screen could be the new norm.

Or not. Ms. deGuzman's video may have landed at one of those cultural moments when people start questioning if something has gone too far and start doing something about it.

Last week, the Unsound music festival in Poland banned fans from recording the event, saying it did not want "instant documentation" and distractions that might take away from the performances. In April, during a show in New York City, Karen O, the lead singer of the rock band the Yeah Yeah Yeahs, told audience members to put away their phones (using an expletive to emphasize her point).

A number of New York restaurants, including Momofuku Ko and Chef's Table at Brooklyn Fare, have prohibited people from photographing their food. (Note to foodies: Your quinoa does not need to be artfully posted with an old-timey look on Instagram.) And, of course, many mothers and fathers who fought to keep the television out of the kitchen may see smartphones as the next threat to dinnertime civility.

In the late 1950s, televisions started to move into the kitchen from the living room, often wheeled up to the dinner table to join the family for supper. And then, TV at the dinner table suddenly became bad manners. Back to the living room the TV went.

"It never really caught on in most U.S. homes," said Lynn Spigel, a professor at the Northwestern University School of Communication and author of the book, "Make Room for TV." "At one point, a company even tried to invent a contraption called the TV Stove, which was both a TV and a stove," she said.

So are smartphones having their TV-in-the-kitchen moment?

"Every experience is being mediated and conceived around how it can be captured and augmented by our devices," said Mathias Crawford, a researcher in human-computer interactions and communications at Stanford University. "No place is this more apparent than our meals, where every portion leading up to, during and after a dining experience is being carved out by particular apps."

People make dinner reservations on OpenTable; check in on Foursquare when they arrive at the restaurant; take a picture of their food to share on Instagram; post on Twitter a joke they hear during the meal; review the restaurant on Yelp; then, finally, coordinate a ride home using Uber.

"If you're wondering when people are going to reject the phone, that will mean they need to reject Silicon Valley's entire concept of how you ought to be dining," Mr. Crawford said. But, he added, it was possible. "Yes, society is changing, but the iPhone is only really six years old, and those changes aren't set in place." Given the overwhelming response to Ms. deGuzman's video, people are at least thinking about those changes.

"It wasn't until this year that I've had these revelations about living in the moment without my phone," Ms. deGuzman said. "I still have my phone with me, but I try to leave it in my purse. Now I find myself just taking in a moment, and I don't have to post a picture about it."

Phone Makers Could Cut Off Drivers. So Why Don't They?

BY MATT RICHTEL | SEPT. 24, 2016

THE COURT FILINGS paint a grisly picture: As Ashley Kubiak sped down a Texas highway in her Dodge Ram truck, she checked her iPhone for messages. Distracted, she crashed into a sport utility vehicle, killing its driver and a passenger and leaving a child paralyzed.

With driving fatalities rising at levels not seen in 50 years, the growing incidence of distracted driving is getting part of the blame. Now a lawsuit related to that 2013 Texas crash is raising a question: Does Apple — or any cellphone maker or wireless company — have a responsibility to prevent devices from being used by drivers in illegal and dangerous ways?

The product liability lawsuit, filed against Apple by families of the victims, contends that Apple knew its phones would be used for texting and did not prevent Ms. Kubiak from texting dangerously. The suit is unlikely to succeed, legal experts said, and a Texas magistrate in August preliminarily recommended the case's dismissal on grounds that it was unlikely that lawyers could prove that the use of the iPhone caused the fatal accident.

Ms. Kubiak was convicted of negligent homicide and sentenced to five years on probation. Her lawyer, Jason Cassel, said she now keeps her phone in the back seat.

"The mere fact she's putting her phone in her back seat in her purse shows she realizes how tempting it is to look down when we get a beep, chime, vibration," Mr. Cassel said. "She never wants to be near the possibility" of being tempted to answer it.

The product liability case has brought to light a piece of evidence that legal and safety experts say puts Apple in a quandary — one it shares with other wireless companies. In Apple's case, the evidence shows, the company has a patent for technology designed to prevent texting while driving, but it has not deployed it.

Apple, Verizon, AT&T and other companies caution about the risks of distracted driving — and they acknowledge that laws and public education aimed at curbing the behavior are not working. It suggests to legal experts that they can foresee that their product can be used for illegal, dangerous and sometimes deadly activity.

AT&T even suggests that the behavior has addictive qualities, meaning drivers cannot help themselves. But the companies — though they offer manual ways to shut down texting on the road — do not deploy technology that takes the decision out of drivers' hands altogether.

"The technology exists — we just don't have the stomach to implement it," said Deborah Hersman, the president of the National Safety Council and the former chairwoman of the National Transportation Safety Board. In 2012, the safety board sent a letter to the wireless industry association urging the companies to prevent drivers from using their phones while driving.

"Technology got us into this situation. Technology will get us out," she said. However, she added, "We're so afraid to tell people what they should do that you can kind of get away with murder under these conditions."

Generally, companies have taken the position that text-blocking technology is embryonic and unreliable. They argue that they cannot shut down a driver's service without the potential of mistakenly shutting off a passenger's phone or that of someone riding on a train or bus.

Instead, companies have taken the approach of simultaneously warning and enabling, a mixed message that underscores a complex swirl of economic, technological and social factors. Perhaps the most pointed question is this: Even if the technology worked to perfection, would people accept having their service blocked? After all, the idea of mobile phone service is to let people communicate on the go.

David Teater, formerly of the National Safety Council and now a private consultant on road safety, who lost his own son to a distracted

RAFA ALVAREZ

driver, said companies clearly feared the consequences of cutting off service for their paying customers. It's an industry, he said, in which one of the most frightening words is "churn" — meaning the loss of a customer to a competitor.

"If you're at Apple or you're at Samsung, do you want to be the first to block texting and driving?" he said. "A customer might say, 'If Apple does it, then my next phone is a Samsung.' "

But to Mr. Teater, that's just an excuse. "If Apple had deployed this technology 10 years ago, there would be more people alive today," he said. "Think about it from a parent's perspective: How would you feel knowing Apple had the ability to prevent your teen from ever texting and driving, and they chose not to?"

APPLE'S LOCKOUT PATENT

In the Apple case in Texas, lawyers who brought the suit had unearthed a fascinating document: a patent filing that Apple made in 2008, which the lawyers said was granted in 2014, for technology that would "lock out" a driver's phone by using sensors to determine if the phone was moving and in use by a driver. If so, it would prevent certain functions, like texting.

In the patent, Apple says such technology is necessary because: "Texting while driving has become so widespread that it is doubtful that law enforcement will have any significant effect on stopping the practice," and "Teens understand that texting while driving is dangerous, but this is often not enough motivation to end the practice."

It is unclear whether Apple has developed the lockout technology.

While texting is on the rise, people are increasingly driving and using Snapchat and Instagram, or taking selfies, or playing Pokémon Go. The phone is at the center of all the activity.

Apple says it has taken other steps to address distracted driving. Its CarPlay integrates with some cars so drivers can use voice commands to control some functions of the car and the phone, including letting them orally compose text messages and listen to incoming ones. The technology, Apple says, "allows you to stay focused on the road."

"We discourage anyone from allowing their iPhone to distract them by typing, reading or interacting with the display while driving," Apple said in response to questions. The company did not directly address whether it could or should shut down phone functions. Rather, it indicated that the responsibility was with the driver.

"For those customers who do not wish to turn off their iPhones or switch into Airplane Mode while driving to avoid distractions, we recommend the easy-to-use Do Not Disturb and Silent Mode features," the statement said.

These approaches put the onus on drivers to make decisions each time they enter a car or receive a message. In addition, voice-activated systems raise other concerns, said David Strayer, an expert on driver attention at the University of Utah, who said he had studied CarPlay and the feature allowed drivers to perform some functions that could take their attention off the road.

"It does not eliminate driver distraction — not even close," Dr. Strayer said.

Technology is already on the market that can block a driver from having to make a decision. One company, Cellcontrol, sells a device that mounts on the dash and that uses high-frequency sound waves to identify a phone's location. If the phone's user is in the driver's seat, the device can lock out prohibited services.

The $129 device, which looks like a small turtle shell, "is very accurate," said Cellcontrol's chief technology officer, Joe Breaux. The hiccup is that the technology can sometimes turn off the phone of a passenger sitting behind the driver.

Apple, in its patent, said it was developing "a process in which handheld computing devices can provide a lockout mechanism without requiring any modifications or additions to the vehicle." It would use motion and scenery sensors to determine if the phone was moving, and its location.

By not putting the technology in place, Apple has "failed in their social responsibility," said Christopher Kutz, a professor at the University of California, Berkeley, School of Law, who specializes in the moral and legal principles of liability. "They should've done it, and even done it at a market risk."

He likened the situation to that of gunmakers who could stop selling high-capacity magazines but choose not to.

At the same time, Mr. Kutz said, there was little precedent for companies to shut off communications services for safety reasons. In other industries, he said, companies have taken such precautions — for instance, some manufacturers have technology that will shut down a machine if a worker does not keep two hands on it.

ADDICTED TO THE PING

In the case of distracted driving, Apple is not the only tech giant recognizing the dangerous behavior and not preventing it. Verizon, like Apple, suggests that current laws are insufficient. "While text messaging is banned for drivers in 46 states and the District of Columbia, many people continue to do it, despite knowing the dangers," Verizon says on a site that promotes free apps and other services available for iPhone and Android that can detect if a phone is being used by a driver and prevent texting.

The Verizon messaging app has a driving mode that, when in use, detects if someone is connected to a car's Bluetooth system and delivers an automatic response to the sender that the recipient is driving, said Kelly Crummey, a Verizon spokeswoman. However, the message still arrives on the recipient's phone, allowing the opportunity to check it, Ms. Crummey said.

That technology suggests it is possible to identify a driver and apply the technology more broadly — to, say, social media — but Ms. Crummey said Verizon didn't have the same kind of control over Facebook, Twitter or other functions. Further, she said, it wouldn't make sense to turn off all phone functions, like maps or navigation, that drivers rely on.

AT&T encourages the use of a free app, Drivemode, that can stop incoming texts. "Everyone knows texting and driving is dangerous, yet when a text message comes in, it's difficult not to respond," AT&T says in promoting the app.

Of course, services like these must be activated by the user and can be bypassed. And AT&T may have identified the reason such solutions don't work: People find themselves so drawn to their devices that elements of addiction are at play.

In fact, AT&T commissioned research by an addiction expert who, in an AT&T news release in 2014, said that using a phone sets off releases of a neurochemical called dopamine that makes it hard to resist the ping. "If that desire for a dopamine fix leads us to check our phones while we're driving, a simple text can turn deadly," David Greenfield, who founded the Center for Internet and Technology Addiction, said in the AT&T news release.

But if the behavior has addictive qualities, can drivers really be expected to police themselves? And should automated blocking be the answer?

“Distracted driving is never O.K.,” AT&T said, adding that it had promoted “It Can Wait,” a public service campaign to discourage texting and driving.

CTIA — the Wireless Association, in its response to questions, said, “Laws, consumer education and technology are pivotal, and we’ve seen this three-prong approach work to stop people from this dangerous practice.”

It hasn’t worked well enough, some say.

Apple, as one of the great cultural influencers, might have the power to change the conversation — to make it fashionable to choose safety over the rush of an incoming text, Mr. Kutz said.

“They’ve made themselves a norm maker,” he said. “With great power comes great responsibility.”

How Evil Is Tech?

OPINION | BY DAVID BROOKS | NOV. 20, 2017

NOT LONG AGO, tech was the coolest industry. Everybody wanted to work at Google, Facebook and Apple. But over the past year the mood has shifted.

Some now believe tech is like the tobacco industry — corporations that make billions of dollars peddling a destructive addiction. Some believe it is like the N.F.L. — something millions of people love, but which everybody knows leaves a trail of human wreckage in its wake.

Surely the people in tech — who generally want to make the world a better place — don't want to go down this road. It will be interesting to see if they can take the actions necessary to prevent their companies from becoming social pariahs.

There are three main critiques of big tech.

The first is that it is destroying the young. Social media promises an end to loneliness but actually produces an increase in solitude and an intense awareness of social exclusion. Texting and other technologies give you more control over your social interactions but also lead to thinner interactions and less real engagement with the world.

As Jean Twenge has demonstrated in book and essay, since the spread of the smartphone, teens are much less likely to hang out with friends, they are less likely to date, they are less likely to work.

Eighth graders who spend 10 or more hours a week on social media are 56 percent more likely to say they are unhappy than those who spend less time. Eighth graders who are heavy users of social media increase their risk of depression by 27 percent. Teens who spend three or more hours a day on electronic devices are 35 percent more likely to have a risk factor for suicide, like making a plan for how to do it. Girls, especially hard hit, have experienced a 50 percent rise in depressive symptoms.

The second critique of the tech industry is that it is causing this addiction on purpose, to make money. Tech companies understand what causes dopamine surges in the brain and they lace their products with "hijacking techniques" that lure us in and create "compulsion loops."

Snapchat has Snapstreak, which rewards friends who snap each other every single day, thus encouraging addictive behavior. News feeds are structured as "bottomless bowls" so that one page view leads down to another and another and so on forever. Most social media sites create irregularly timed rewards; you have to check your device compulsively because you never know when a burst of social affirmation from a Facebook like may come.

The third critique is that Apple, Amazon, Google and Facebook are near monopolies that use their market power to invade the private lives of their users and impose unfair conditions on content creators and smaller competitors. The political assault on this front is gaining steam. The left is attacking tech companies because they are mammoth corporations; the right is attacking them because they are culturally progressive. Tech will have few defenders on the national scene.

Obviously, the smart play would be for the tech industry to get out in front and clean up its own pollution. There are activists like Tristan Harris of Time Well Spent, who is trying to move the tech world in the right directions. There are even some good engineering responses. I use an app called Moment to track and control my phone usage.

The big breakthrough will come when tech executives clearly acknowledge the central truth: Their technologies are extremely useful for the tasks and pleasures that require shallower forms of consciousness, but they often crowd out and destroy the deeper forms of consciousness people need to thrive.

Online is a place for human contact but not intimacy. Online is a place for information but not reflection. It gives you the first stereotypical thought about a person or a situation, but it's hard to carve out time and space for the third, 15th and 43rd thought.

Online is a place for exploration but discourages cohesion. It grabs control of your attention and scatters it across a vast range of diverting things. But we are happiest when we have brought our lives to a point, when we have focused attention and will on one thing, wholeheartedly with all our might.

Rabbi Abraham Joshua Heschel wrote that we take a break from the distractions of the world not as a rest to give us more strength to dive back in, but as the climax of living. “The seventh day is a palace in time which we build. It is made of soul, joy and reticence,” he said. By cutting off work and technology we enter a different state of consciousness, a different dimension of time and a different atmosphere, a “mine where the spirit’s precious metal can be found.”

Imagine if instead of claiming to offer us the best things in life, tech merely saw itself as providing efficiency devices. Its innovations can save us time on lower-level tasks so we can get offline and there experience the best things in life.

Imagine if tech pitched itself that way. That would be an amazing show of realism and, especially, humility, which these days is the ultimate and most disruptive technology.

DAVID BROOKS is an Op-Ed columnist for The New York Times.

Tech Backlash Grows as Investors Press Apple to Act on Children's Use

BY DAVID GELLES | JAN. 8, 2018

A CREATOR OF the iPhone called the device "addictive."

A Twitter founder said the "internet is broken."

An early Facebook investor raised questions about the social network's impact on children's brains.

Now, two of the biggest investors on Wall Street have asked Apple to study the health effects of its products and to make it easier for parents to limit their children's use of iPhones and iPads.

Once uncritically hailed for their innovation and economic success, Silicon Valley companies are under fire from all sides, facing calls to take more responsibility for their role in everything from election meddling and hate speech to physical health and internet addiction.

"Companies have a role to play in helping to address these issues," said Barry Rosenstein, managing partner of Jana Partners, an investment firm that wrote an open letter to Apple this weekend pushing it to look at its products' health effects, especially on children. "As more and more founders of the biggest tech companies are acknowledging today, the days of just throwing technology out there and washing your hands of the potential impact are over."

The backlash against big tech has been growing for months. Facebook and Twitter are under scrutiny for their roles in enabling Russian meddling in the 2016 presidential election and for facilitating abusive behavior. Google was hit with a record antitrust fine in Europe for improperly exploiting its market power.

But until now, Apple had escaped largely unscathed, and concerns about the deleterious effects of excessive technology use have not been among the most pressing matters for Silicon Valley executives.

Jana, an activist hedge fund, wrote its letter with Calstrs, the California State Teachers' Retirement System, which manages the pensions of California's public-school teachers. When such investors pressure companies to change their behavior, it is typically with the goal of lifting a sagging stock price. In this case, Jana and Calstrs said they were trying to raise awareness about an issue they cared deeply about, adding that if Apple was proactive about making changes, it could help the business.

"We believe the long-term health of its youngest customers and the health of society, our economy and the company itself are inextricably linked," the investors said in the letter. Jana, which is often vilified for its aggressive focus on short-term profits, also said it would be raising a fund this year that would engage in more such campaigns, an effort that could help soften its image.

Whatever the motivations, the two large investors are tapping into the growing anxiety among parents about their children's preoccupation with devices, at the expense of activities like reading and sports.

"Over the past 10 years, there's been a bottom-up backlash," said Sherry Turkle, a professor at the Massachusetts Institute of Technology and the author of "Alone Together: Why We Expect More From Technology and Less From Each Other." "You see it in things like people not sending their kids to schools that use iPads, and kids telling their parents to put their phones down."

For years, researchers have been sounding the alarm over the ubiquity of mobile phones and social media. A 2015 study by Common Sense Media, a research group that studies technology use, found that more than half of teenagers spent upward of four hours a day looking at screens, and that for a quarter of teenagers, the figure was more than eight hours. In another survey, in 2016, half the teenagers said they felt addicted to their mobile devices.

"These things can be incredibly addictive," said Tony Fadell, a former Apple executive who helped create the iPod and iPhone. "It's amazing, but there are a lot of unintended consequences."

A growing roster of prominent technology executives have grown worried about the creations that brought them fame and fortune.

Sean Parker, an early investor in Facebook, reflected on the sprawling influence of the social network. "It literally changes your relationship with society, with each other," he said in an interview with Axios in November. "It probably interferes with productivity in weird ways. God only knows what it's doing to our children's brains."

Evan Williams, one of the founders of Twitter, last year lamented the degree to which the messaging service had become a bastion for hateful speech. "The internet is broken," he said.

Chamath Palihapitiya, an early Facebook executive and the chief executive of Social Capital, a venture capital firm, said in November that he felt "tremendous guilt" about his role in building the social network.

"The short term, dopamine-driven feedback loops that we have created are destroying how society works," he said. "No civil discourse, no cooperation, misinformation, mistruth. And it's not an American problem. This is not about Russian ads. This is a global problem."

By going after Apple, Jana and Calstrs, which together own about $2 billion worth of the company's stock, have selected the tech giant that is perhaps least dependent on its users' time. Because Apple makes most of its money selling hardware, rather than through digital advertising, it theoretically could afford to encourage its users to spend less time with its products.

"Apple's business model is not predicated on excessive use of your products," Jana and Calstrs said in their letter to the company.

For this reason, said Ms. Turkle, the M.I.T. professor, "it turns out that Apple is the company best positioned to act."

In a statement, Apple said that the parental controls already on its devices "lead the industry" and that "we think deeply about how our products are used and the impact they have on users and the people around them."

"We take this responsibility very seriously," the statement continued, "and we are committed to meeting and exceeding our customers' expectations, especially when it comes to protecting kids."

Fears about technology addiction are not new. The BlackBerry, an early smartphone, was nicknamed "CrackBerry." Adam Alter, a social psychologist and the author of "Irresistible: The Rise of Addictive Technology and the Business of Keeping Us Hooked," documents instances of internet addiction spanning the globe.

But some tech executives now acknowledge that far from being an accident, their products were designed to be addictive.

Mr. Parker said that when Facebook was getting started, the thought process was about "how do we consume as much of your time and conscious attention as possible?"

Mr. Palihapitiya said as Facebook was rapidly growing, "in the back, deep, deep recesses of our minds, we kind of knew something bad could happen."

Mr. Fadell said that at the time Apple was designing the iPhone, "we had no idea this was going to happen." But, he added, people today are simply spending too much time looking at their phones.

"Now it needs to be addressed," he said. "It's been 10 years in the making."

Even Mark Zuckerberg, the chief executive of Facebook and usually a staunch defender of his company's influence, has appeared more reflective in recent days.

"The world feels anxious and divided, and Facebook has a lot of work to do — whether it's protecting our community from abuse and hate, defending against interference by nation states, or making sure that time spent on Facebook is time well spent," he said in a Facebook post last week. "My personal challenge for 2018 is to focus on fixing these important issues."

Your Kid's Phone Is Not Like a Cigarette

OPINION | BY ANYA KAMENETZ | MARCH 3, 2018

A NEW NATIONAL ad campaign, "Truth About Tech," is designed to expose the ways that platforms like YouTube, Snapchat and Facebook are harmful to children and to "protect young minds from digital manipulation and exploitation."

Organized by the nonprofits Common Sense and the Center for Humane Technology, it has been compared by its organizers to the "Truth" anti-tobacco campaign, which, beginning in 1999, rolled out ads — including images of body bags placed outside a major tobacco company to represent the number of people killed by tobacco each day — that are credited with helping to slash teenage smoking rates.

"Think of it like the Truth campaign for cigarettes. If you remember the 1990s TV ads, it was not saying, 'Hey, this is going to have this bad health consequences for you if you smoke,' " Tristan Harris, the founder and executive director of the Center for Humane Technology, said in a February interview about the campaign with Vox.com. "The Truth campaign was about telling you the truth about how they design it deliberately to be addictive."

But an anti-tobacco campaign is not an ideal model for the effort to make technology safer for children. Because while there's plenty of concern about overuse of technology among young people, the actual evidence of addictiveness and harm is much more complex than it was in the case of cigarettes.

Sure, there are treatment facilities for adolescents who are hooked on devices, and psychologists use terms like "problematic media use" in describing a small percentage of people who seem to prefer screens to people. But experts are split over the question of whether internet addiction is a legitimate stand-alone disorder.

A Common Sense spokeswoman, Corbie Kiernan, told me, "We use the term 'addiction' colloquially, not diagnostically," in response to parents' concerns. Of course, only a rank apologist would deny that there is cause for concern about the role mobile devices are playing in children's and young people's lives. Media habits are shifting fast: The amount of time children 8 years old and younger spend on phones or tablets has increased tenfold in just five years, according to a 2017 study by Common Sense. The organization also found that 42 percent of children under 8 already have their own mobile device. That number was less than 1 percent in 2011.

While those of us who grew up before smartphones can agree that these changes are jarring, the extent of the harm done to kids by more screens than we could ever have imagined is not at all clear. The real "truth about tech" is that there just isn't enough research on this yet. For example, when I asked Victor C. Strasburger of the American Academy of Pediatrics how the organization arrived at its "no screens before age 2" recommendation, he said that later studies supported the guidance but admitted that at the time it was put into effect, "there was no evidence. None. We made it up." (The group has since changed its stance, maintaining that it's best to keep the youngest children away from screens, but making an exception for live video chat.)

An open letter in January from Apple shareholders calling for parental controls and more research into the effects of heavy use of mobile devices on youth was also based on fairly flimsy evidence. For example, the letter cited the work of a psychologist who analyzed large surveys to find that heavy electronic device use among teenagers is correlated with reports of loneliness, depression, anxiety and the increased presence of suicide risk factors. But this connection does not prove which way the causal arrow points. Perhaps teenagers who are under emotional duress gravitate toward their phones. Maybe they have parents with troubles of their own who are less capable of supervising them.

TOMI UM

The science here is nothing like the kind that fueled the Truth campaign against cigarettes. For that reason alone, those working to make tech safer for kids can't emulate that campaign.

The activism that led to greater automobile safety is a much better model. Without the smoking-gun science that can win a legal battle against a deep-pocketed industry, there's no role in the campaign for tech safety for someone like Mike Moore, the former Mississippi attorney general who sued 13 tobacco companies. But there is a need for a modern-day Ralph Nader, the fiery young author who, in 1965, when his book "Unsafe at Any Speed" came out, accused automobile manufacturers of failing to make cars as safe as possible.

Nonprofits committed to addressing the impact of technology on children could also look to Candace Lightner for inspiration. She founded Mothers Against Drunk Driving, which lobbied Congress to strengthen laws and implored people through public campaigns to voluntarily hand over the car keys when intoxicated.

When it came to tobacco, the solution was simple: Quit or don't start smoking. That's not the case here. Phones, tablets and other devices that have caused so much concern have more in common with cars than with cigarettes; unlike tobacco, they are essential tools that can be used in a healthy way.

With this in mind, activists shouldn't simply vilify the tech industry — they should goad it toward accountability as Mr. Nader, Ms. Lightner and others did with the auto industry. They need to summon the art of moral suasion to create powerful cultural memes, like that of the "designated driver," to push us to use tech more safely. (Especially, by the way, in cars. Designated texters, anyone?)

The smartphone equivalents of seatbelts, airbags and anti-lock brakes may currently be in research and development. Just one example: Gabe Zichermann, a gamification expert, is developing an app called Onward that turns the process of quitting your phone into a game.

Parents should grow into their roles as advocates for change in the tech industry, as they did with car safety. Moms and dads have a lot of clout. Senators found it hard to look Ms. Lightner in the eye and explain why the driver who killed her daughter hadn't received a harsher punishment the first time he was caught driving drunk. Thanks in part to her advocacy, the National Minimum Drinking Age Act was passed in 1984.

To be fair, the Truth About Tech campaign is seeking to raise awareness among parents and to address the industry. Its "Road Map for Kids' Digital Well-Being" includes calls to "build public awareness" and "provide tools to educate parents, teachers and kids."

Mr. Harris, of the Center for Humane Technology, who studied persuasive technology and then spent time as a digital ethicist at Google, now pushes for social networks to adopt less nefarious business models. He also suggests a simple method of making your phone less compelling: Set it to grayscale.

The campaign, and the concerned Apple shareholders, should focus on these kinds of approaches and avoid imitating the fight against Big Tobacco by creating a moral panic about the specter of addiction. After all, the goal is to inspire a cultural shift around technology like the one we saw around car safety — not to snuff out kids' use of devices altogether.

ANYA KAMENETZ is the author of "The Art of Screen Time: How Your Family Can Balance Digital Media and Real Life."

Parenting the Fortnite Addict

BY LISA DAMOUR | APRIL 30, 2018

EVERY SO OFTEN a game comes along that conquers the hearts, minds and thumbs of gamers everywhere. Fortnite: Battle Royale is the latest victor in this category. According to a report last week from the market research firm SuperData, the game generated $223 million in March, and it begins a new season — with a new theme and a few other changes — on May 1.

Like a cross between Minecraft and the Hunger Games, Fortnite drops 100 competitors on an island and requires them to scavenge for weapons and other resources, build defensive structures and vanquish opponents in a quest to become the last player standing. The game itself is free and playable on game systems, computers and mobile phones alike, but players pay for accessories and costumes for their characters.

Not surprisingly, middle and high schools are finding themselves at odds with students who surreptitiously play the game throughout the day. The game is also popular with adults, including Major League Baseball players, who compellingly bring an element of the game into real life through victory dances on the field based on dances from the game. For parents bewildered by the sense that the game has swallowed their children, especially since the mobile phone version was released in late March, here's some information that may help.

IT'S A SOCIAL EXPERIENCE ...

While Fortnite can be played solo, it is often a social experience as friends can team up in pairs or fours. If they're not together physically, they communicate — over FaceTime, a headset linked to a game system, or the like — to coordinate strategy, alert teammates to threats, root for one another and trade banter.

Young people use the game to connect in a variety of ways. Owen Purcell, age 11, of Shaker Heights, Ohio, is known for his fort-building prowess, so he is often recruited onto teams formed by his older brothers and their high school and college-aged friends. When he's not lending his talents to the older set, Owen collaborates with selected friends his own age: "It's more fun with your friends, but it depends on the friends. It's only fun with real friends who you really want to be with."

Fortnite does, to be sure, involve firearms, and is recommended for ages 13 and up. But its graphics are free of blood and gore. And though adults may worry that shooting games cultivate aggression, C. Shawn Green, an associate professor of psychology at the University of Wisconsin-Madison who researches video games, notes that, "there's really no evidence that playing a violent video game would take someone who has absolutely no violent tendencies and suddenly make them violent."

Research does, however, confirm that action video games cultivate the spatial skills needed in advanced mathematics and engineering.

And there's another wrinkle that may appeal to kids and parents alike: At least one college has announced it is offering scholarship money to skilled Fortnite players.

... BUT IT IS BUILT TO BE ADDICTIVE

Fortnite incorporates much of what game designers know about how to ensure a captive audience. Some of what hooks players is obvious: it has quality graphics, a sense of humor and advances rapidly. But it also includes stealth habit-forming features, such as an element of luck that keeps players coming back for more. As with gambling, it's hard to walk away if you believe that good fortune is always just around the corner.

When players learn how to survive longer into the game, they may likewise be drawn in by the powerful "near miss" phenomenon. Instead of feeling as if they've lost, players may feel as if they *nearly* won. "It's like an adrenaline rush if you almost win," says Miles Weiskopf, age 14, of University Heights, Ohio, "you feel like 'I gotta play again.' "

And the heavily social aspect of Fortnite serves to make the game even more compelling. As Laurence Steinberg, a professor of psychology at Temple University and a leading expert on adolescence explains, "Whatever kids do, they enjoy it more when they're with other kids."

SETTING LIMITS IN A POSITIVE WAY

Given the game's gripping power, young people may need help limiting their involvement with it. So how should parents step in? Instead of being *against* playing Fortnite, some adults position themselves as being *for* other important activities, such as completing homework, being physically active, participating in family life and getting enough sleep. As Dr. Green notes, "there is value to setting limits to how much a young person can do one thing because it's useful for kids to have a variety of experiences and to engage in lots of different intellectual activities."

There's another reason parents might want to insist that all screen time (game playing included) comes after other priorities have been addressed: because there are many ways to engage with Fortnite beyond actually playing it. Enthusiasts may devote hours to watching streaming videos of highly skilled gamers, studying highlight reels posted on YouTube and tracking the game's strong social media presence and following among celebrities like Drake.

Parents might reduce some friction at home by talking with their family gamer about how best to keep Fortnite in check. Davida Pines of Waban, Mass., and her 14-year-old son, Noah, found that a hard stop didn't work because, as Noah explained to his mother, "pulling out with no warning is like leaving a soccer game or another team sport just when the team might need you most."

They now agree on a rough period of time for playing. At a certain point, Dr. Pines alerts Noah that he's on his last game, knowing that a single game can take less than a minute for a gamer ambushed by an adversary who quickly finds a rifle, or not more than 20 minutes for the competitor who wins.

The game itself may even provide a carrot adults can use to their advantage. Though Fortnite is free, participants have the option of purchasing costumes known as "skins" to customize the look of their combatant. Parents of players who are jonesing for a skin might consider offering to buy one as a reward for a period of good compliance with the household technology rules.

Adults who are catching up to Fortnite shouldn't hesitate to ask young people about the game. I have found that many teenagers love to talk about it with anyone who's willing. And while learning about the details of this latest craze may not be at the top of every parent's agenda, learning more about why the game captivates one's kid just might be.

LISA DAMOUR is a psychologist in Shaker Heights, Ohio, and the author of "Untangled: Guiding Teenage Girls Through the Seven Transitions Into Adulthood."

The Big Myth About Teenage Anxiety

OPINION | BY RICHARD A. FRIEDMAN | SEPT. 7, 2018

Relax: The digital age is not wrecking your kid's brain.

WE HEAR A lot these days that modern digital technology is rewiring the brains of our teenagers, making them anxious, worried and unable to focus.

Don't panic; things are really not this dire.

Despite news reports to the contrary, there is little evidence of an epidemic of anxiety disorders in teenagers. This is for the simple reason that the last comprehensive and representative survey of psychiatric disorders among American youth was conducted more than a decade ago, according to Kathleen Ries Merikangas, chief of the Genetic Epidemiology Research Branch at the National Institute of Mental Health.

There are a few surveys reporting increased anxiety in adolescents, but these are based on self-reported measures — from kids or their parents — which tend to overestimate the rates of disorders because they detect mild symptoms, not clinically significant syndromes.

So what's behind the idea that teenagers are increasingly worried and nervous? One possibility is that these stories are the leading edge of a wave of anxiety disorders that has yet to be captured in epidemiological surveys. Or maybe anxiety rates have risen, but only in the select demographic groups — the privileged ones — that receive a lot of media attention.

But it's more likely that the epidemic is simply a myth. The more interesting question is why it has been so widely accepted as fact.

One reason, I believe, is that parents have bought into the idea that digital technology — smartphones, video games and the like — are neurobiologically and psychologically toxic. If you believe this, it seems intuitive that the generations growing up with these ubiquitous technologies are destined to suffer from psychological problems. But this dubious notion comes from a handful of studies with serious limitations.

Some studies report an association between increased time spent on electronic communication and screens and lower levels of psychological well-being. The problem is that they show only correlation. It is entirely possible that teenagers who are more anxious and unhappy to start with are more drawn to smartphones to deflect their negative emotions than their better-adjusted peers.

Another group of studies use M.R.I. to examine the brains of young people who are "addicted" to internet video games, and report various structural and functional differences. For example, one study reported that a group of 17 teenagers with online gaming "addiction" had microstructural changes in various brain regions compared with a control group.

But, once again, these studies cannot tell us whether the brain abnormalities are the result of excessive internet use, or a pre-existing risk factor for it.

What about the claim that smartphones can be literally addicting, like illicit drugs? This appears to be based on a few M.R.I. studies that show that kids with online gaming "addiction" have enhanced activation in their brain's reward pathway when shown gaming images.

No surprise there. If I scan your brain while showing you whatever it is that turns you on — sex, chocolate or money, say — your reward pathway will light up like a Christmas tree. But that hardly means you are addicted to these things.

The real question is whether digital technology can produce the enduring changes in the brain that addictive drugs do. There is little evidence that this is the case. And while an alcoholic deprived of his drink can go into life-threatening withdrawal, I have yet to see an adolescent in the emergency room with smartphone withdrawal — just a sullen teenager who wants his device back.

Considering all this, why do so many parents still insist that their teenager has a problem with anxiety? I fear that it reflects a cultural shift toward pathologizing everyday levels of distress.

There is a difference between an anxiety disorder and everyday anxiety. The first impairs people's ability to function because they suffer from excessive anxiety even when there is little or nothing to be anxious about. The second is a perfectly normal and rational response to real stress. Teenagers — and people of all ages — will and *should* feel anxious occasionally.

Some would argue that young people today are more worried because the world is now in a more parlous state, what with intense competition for college and the lingering effects of the Great Recession, among other factors. Sure, but then that anxiety is an appropriate response to life's challenges — not a disorder.

Of course this is anecdotal, but as a psychiatrist, I haven't seen an increase in the number of patients suffering from true anxiety disorders, who need therapy and often medication to keep their affliction in check. What I have noticed is that more of my young patients worry a lot about things that don't seem so serious, and then worry about their worry.

A few patients in their early 20s, for example, were under a lot of stress at work, and were alarmed by a few nights of poor sleep. None of them were clinically depressed, yet they were convinced that their insomnia would seriously impair their work or make them physically sick. All were surprised and easily reassured when I told them there was little cause for concern. Why, I wondered, didn't they know this without me?

I got a clue when, for the first time a few years ago, I received a phone call from the mother of a teenage patient. She was concerned that her son was unhappy in the wake of a breakup with his girlfriend and asked me to call him to "check on him."

Since there was nothing more than a vague worry about his unhappiness — a perfectly normal response to romantic disappointment — I told her that he could always contact me if he needed to.

Since then, I have received similar calls from parents worried about their teenagers' ability to handle everyday adversity — for example, underperforming on a high-stakes exam or failing to get a summer job.

These well-meaning parents are conveying to their kids that their emotional responses to difficult but ordinary experiences are not to be taken in stride, but viewed as something needing clinical attention.

The truth is that our brains are both more resilient and more resistant to change than we think. The myth of an epidemic of anxiety disorder rooted in a generation's overexposure to digital technology reveals an exaggerated idea about just how open to influence our brains really are.

Yes, our brain has evolved to learn and extract critical information from the environment, but there are limits to neuroplasticity. Even when we are young and impressionable, our brains have molecular and structural brakes that control the degree to which they can be rewired by experience (and these tighten as we age).

This is a good thing; without these limits, we would be at risk of overwriting — and losing — accumulated knowledge that is critical to our survival, to say nothing of our identity.

It's good to keep in mind that the advent of new technology typically provokes medical and moral panic. Remember all those warnings that TV would cause brain rot? Never happened. The notion that the brain is a tabula rasa that can be easily transformed by digital technology is, as yet, the stuff of science fiction.

So don't assume that there's something wrong with your kid every time he's anxious or upset. Our teenagers — and their brains — are up to the challenges of modern life.

RICHARD A. FRIEDMAN is a professor of clinical psychiatry and the director of the psychopharmacology clinic at the Weill Cornell Medical College, and a contributing opinion writer.

CHAPTER 4

Who Wins the Digital Race?

The powerful lure of advancing tech continues to influence society. Sexting and gaming have become normal features of teenage life. A number of people suffer ill effects from overuse of tech, from psychological difficulties to physical effects like tendinitis and tendinosis. The Silicon Valley creators of Internet superstars Facebook and Google have joined in a coalition to mediate the negative effects of tech.

What They're Saying About Sexting

BY THE NEW YORK TIMES | MARCH 26, 2011

THE NEW YORK TIMES interviewed teenagers individually and in two focus groups. The first, in Manhattan, was organized by the Anti-Defamation League, which offers cyberbullying prevention programs. The second, with students from Lower Merion, a Philadelphia suburb, was coordinated by Stephanie Newberg, a therapist who works with adolescents, and Paula Singer, a community organizer.

The following quotes from the sessions and interviews have been edited and condensed.

Q. *Is sexting ever O.K.?*

Saif, 18, Brooklyn: It's a way to express your feelings. If a guy and a girl are in love, instead of saying it face to face, they can say it through technology.

Kathy, 17, Queens: There's a positive side to sexting. You can't get pregnant from it, and you can't transmit S.T.D.'s. It's a kind of safe sex.

Q. *How common is sexting at your school?*

Mei, 16, Staten Island: People call us the nerd school. My friends wouldn't think sexting is all right. But even with the popular kids, it's not acceptable.

Kathy: At my school, if you like a boy and you want to get his attention, you know what you have to do. When I was with my last boyfriend I refused to sext and I would go through his iPod and find pictures of girls' breasts, and in weird ways that I never wanted to see. And they were all girls in my school.

Farrah, 17, Lower Merion: People don't think it's that big of a deal anymore.

Q. *Do boys sext as often as girls?*

Farrah: No. But the guys who get caught sexting are the cockier ones who just like to show off what they're working with.

Q. *Why do girls sext?*

Zoe, 18, Lower Merion: A freshman girl doesn't consciously want to be a slut, but she wants to be liked and she likes attention from the older boys. They'll text to her, "Hey, hottie," and it will progress from there.

Joe, 17, Lower Merion: I don't think those girls are insecure. I think they're confident, and they know they're hot.

Rachel, 18, Philadelphia: A girl thinks, "I know I've been warned against it, but this is something I want to share with my boyfriend, and he's different."

Q. *How are texts used differently from photos in sexting?*

William, 18, Lower Merion: Photo sexting is done more in middle school when you just get this technology and you're horny.

Farrah: As you get older, kids use raunchy texts more. They're things kids wouldn't want to say in person. But they can really send the wrong message.

William: If a girl sent me a picture of her boobs, well, obviously I'd like to show it to some friends. But I wouldn't show them a raunchy text from her because that would be awkward. Sexually charged language is more intimate, more private.

Zoe: We see virtual images all day long, so if someone sends you an image, it loses the identity of the person. It's just a picture.

William: And usually the face is not in it.

Q. *Why do sexts go viral?*

Rachel: In eighth grade, four girls were having a sleepover and they took off their clothes, covered themselves with whipped cream and sent pictures to boys of themselves licking it off. People forwarded it because it was gossip and scandalous. In middle school, that's really appealing.

Q. *How often do they go viral, really?*

Nate, 16, Lower Merion: About three photos go viral each year and a third of the school sees them. The kids who receive them are in the alpha social group, and they send it to their friends. But everyone hears about them.

Q. *To what extent do parents know about sexting?*

Glenn, 18, Long Island: I didn't tell my parents I was doing this focus group because they don't know what sexting is, and it would be awkward to talk about it.

Kathy: My mom and I talk about everything.

Q. *Did you know that sexting under 18 is illegal?*

Saif: There's a law? I didn't know that. How would you catch somebody when everyone does it?

Just One More Game . . .

BY SAM ANDERSON | APRIL 4, 2012

Angry Birds, Farmville and Other Hyperaddictive 'Stupid Games'

IN 1989, AS communism was beginning to crumble across Eastern Europe, just a few months before protesters started pecking away at the Berlin Wall, the Japanese game-making giant Nintendo reached across the world to unleash upon America its own version of freedom. The new product was the Game Boy — a handheld, battery-powered plastic slab that promised to set gamers loose, after all those decades of sweaty bondage, from the tyranny of rec rooms and pizza parlors and arcades.

The unit came bundled with a single cartridge: Tetris, a simple but addictive puzzle game whose goal was to rotate falling blocks — over and over and over and over and over and over and over — in order to build the most efficient possible walls. (Well, it was complicated. You were both building walls and not building walls; if you built them right, the walls disappeared, thereby ceasing to be walls.) This turned out to be a perfect symbiosis of game and platform. Tetris's graphics were simple enough to work on the Game Boy's small gray-scale screen; its motion was slow enough not to blur; its action was a repetitive, storyless puzzle that could be picked up, with no loss of potency, at any moment, in any situation. The pairing went on to sell more than 70 million copies, spreading the freedom of compulsive wall-building into every breakfast nook and bank line in the country.

And so a tradition was born: a tradition I am going to call (half descriptively, half out of revenge for all the hours I've lost to them) "stupid games." In the nearly 30 years since Tetris's invention — and especially over the last five, with the rise of smartphones — Tetris and its offspring (Angry Birds, Bejeweled, Fruit Ninja, etc.) have colonized our pockets and our brains and shifted the entire economic model of the video-game industry. Today we are living, for better and worse, in a world of stupid games.

Game-studies scholars (there are such things) like to point out that games tend to reflect the societies in which they are created and played. Monopoly, for instance, makes perfect sense as a product of the 1930s — it allowed anyone, in the middle of the Depression, to play at being a tycoon. Risk, released in the 1950s, is a stunningly literal expression of cold-war realpolitik. Twister is the translation, onto a game board, of the mid-1960s sexual revolution. One critic called it "sex in a box."

Tetris was invented exactly when and where you would expect — in a Soviet computer lab in 1984 — and its game play reflects this origin. The enemy in Tetris is not some identifiable villain (Donkey Kong, Mike Tyson, Carmen Sandiego) but a faceless, ceaseless, reasonless force that threatens constantly to overwhelm you, a churning production of blocks against which your only defense is a repetitive, meaningless sorting. It is bureaucracy in pure form, busywork with no aim or end, impossible to avoid or escape. And the game's final insult is that it annihilates free will. Despite its obvious futility, somehow we can't make ourselves stop rotating blocks. Tetris, like all the stupid games it spawned, forces us to choose to punish ourselves.

In 2009, 25 years after the invention of Tetris, a nearly bankrupt Finnish company called Rovio hit upon a similarly perfect fusion of game and device: Angry Birds. The game involves launching peevish birds at green pigs hiding inside flimsy structures. Its basic mechanism — using your index finger to pull back a slingshot, over and over and over and over and over and over — was the perfect use of the new technology of the touch screen: simple enough to lure a suddenly immense new market of casual gamers, satisfying enough to hook them.

Within months, Angry Birds became the most popular game on the iPhone, then spread across every other available platform. Today it has been downloaded, in its various forms, more than 700 million times. It has also inspired a disturbingly robust merchandising empire: films, T-shirts, novelty slippers, even plans for Angry Birds "activity parks" featuring play equipment for kids. For months, a sign outside my local auto-repair shop promised, "Free Angry Birds pen with service." The game's latest iteration, Angry Birds Space, appeared a couple weeks ago with a promotional push from Wal-Mart, T-Mobile, National Geographic Books, MTV and NASA. (There was an announcement on the International Space Station.) Angry Birds, it seems, is our Tetris: the string of digital prayer beads that our entire culture can twiddle in moments of rapture or anxiety — economic, political or existential.

I RESISTED BUYING an iPhone for what felt like several decades (it was, in biological Earth time, four years), because I was afraid of the power of its games. I spent my formative years becoming fluent in, and addicted to, the video games of the '80s and early '90s — the industry-redefining stretch from roughly Mario Brothers to Mortal Kombat. You could say that video games and I went through adolescence together. As I shed my exoskeleton of fat, Nintendo's blocky pixels started to fuse into sleek 64-bit curves; as my voice lowered, video games' plinky soundtracks matured into little symphonies; as my social circle expanded beyond my little clutch of sweaty and foul-mouthed friends, the market for video games expanded into (or at least toward) similarly new demographics: adults, girls.

At some point late in my teens, in a spasm of post-adolescent resolve, I decided to renounce video games forever. They had, I recognized, a scary power over me — an opium kind of power — and I was hoping to cultivate other, more impressive ways of spending my time. I had aspirations of capital "c" culture, and so I started pouring my attention into books, a quieter and more socially respected form of escapism. I knew that, if I had daily access to video games, I would spend literally every day playing them, forever. So I cut myself off, more or less cold turkey, and as a result I was more or less happy and productive.

Then, midway through the dark forest of my adult life, the iPhone came out. This presented a unique problem. It was not only a phone and a camera and a compass and a map and a tiny window through which to see the entire Internet — it was also a pocket-size game console three times as sophisticated as anything I grew up with. My wife, who had never been a serious gamer, got one and became addicted, almost immediately, to a form of off-brand digital Scrabble called Words With Friends. Before long she was playing 6 or 10 games at a time, against people all over the world. Sometimes I would lose her in the middle of a conversation: her phone would go *brinnng* or *pwomp* or *dernalernadern-dern*, and she would look away from me, midsentence, to see if her opponent had set her up for a triple word score. I tried to stay good-humored. I told her I was going to invent something called the iPaddle: a little screen-size wooden paddle that I would slide in front of her phone whenever she drifted away, on the back of which, upside-down so she could read them, would be inscribed humanist messages from the analog world: "I love you" or "Be here now."

Inevitably, my high-minded detachment didn't last long. About a year ago, unable to resist the rising cultural tide and wanting (I convinced myself) a camera with which to take pictures of my children, I gave in and bought an iPhone. For a while I used it only to read, to e-mail and to take pictures. Then I downloaded chess, which seemed wholesome enough — the PBS of time-wasters. But chess turned out to be a gateway game. Once I formed the habit of finding reliable game joy in my omnipresent pocket-window, my inner 13-year-old reasserted himself. I downloaded horribly titled games like Bix (in which you steer a dot in a box between other dots in a box) and MiZoo (in which you make patterns out of exotic cartoon animal heads). These led to better, more time-consuming games — Orbital, Bejeweled, Touch Physics, Anodia — which led to even better games: Peggle, Little Wings. One tiny masterpiece, Plants vs. Zombies, ate up, I'm going to guess, a full "Anna Karenina" of my leisure time. One day while I was playing it (I think I had just discovered that if you set up your garlic and your money-flowers exactly right, you could sit there racking up coins all day), my wife reminded me of my old joke about the iPaddle. This made me inexplicably angry.

And so video games were back in my life.

MY PLUNGE INTO the world of stupid games was not mine alone: over the last few years, millions of people have been sucked into that vortex. As the venture capitalist John Doerr told Vanity Fair last summer, "These games are not for everyone, it's true, but it's for more of everyone than anything else I know." In 2011, Rovio's chief executive claimed that Angry Birds players were spending 200 million minutes inside the game every day — a number that seems simultaneously absurd and plausible. A number like that can't tell us, however, about the quality of those minutes; how many of them were fun or fulfilling or even intentional.

Humans have always played stupid games. Dice are older than recorded history. Ancient Egyptians played a board game called Senet, which archaeologists believe was something like sacred backgammon. We have rock-paper-scissors, tick-tack-toe, checkers, dominoes and solitaire — small, abstract games in which sets of simple rules play out in increasingly complex scenarios. (Chess, you might say, is the king of stupid games: the tide line where stupid games meet genius.)

But pre-Tetris games were different in a primal way. They required human opponents or at least equipment — the manipulation of three-dimensional objects in space. When you sat down to play them, chances were you meant to sit down and play them.

Stupid games, on the other hand, are rarely occasions in themselves. They are designed to push their way through the cracks of other occasions. We play them incidentally, ambivalently, compulsively, almost accidentally. They're less an activity in our day than a blank space in our day; less a pursuit than a distraction from other pursuits. You glance down to check your calendar and suddenly it's 40 minutes later and there's only one level left before you jump to the next stage, so you might as well just launch another bird.

For most of the last 25 years, it was easy to avoid playing these kinds of games. The game industry operated on a Hollywood model: big companies invested heavily in the production of what came to be known as "Triple-A" games, the industry equivalent of summer blockbusters, which were designed to be played mainly on consoles (PlayStation, Xbox, Dreamcast and GameCube). Like summer blockbusters, these games usually involved quests and wars and bombastic special effects that made them appealing to teenage boys. A Triple-A game could have a production budget of $25 million, with hundreds of developers working on it for years at a time and a $50 million marketing campaign to ensure its ubiquity upon release. On the strength of this model, video-game revenue more than doubled from 1996 to 2005, with the vast majority of that wealth coming from a tiny sliver of blue-chip franchises like Halo, World of Warcraft, Call of Duty and Battlefield. There was a downside, however, to the Hollywood model, which was that the industry fell prey to all the complaints people had been making for decades about Hollywood. The huge budgets and time investments created a conservative, risk-averse culture. Everything was about imitations, spinoffs, prequels, sequels and even subsequels. There is not only a Halo 3 but an entirely separate game called Halo 3: ODST. (It stands for Orbital Drop Shock Troopers.) Meanwhile, the juggernaut companies (Microsoft, Electronic Arts, Rockstar Games) dominated the market so thoroughly that independent game designers, who might have refreshed things, had no practical way to get their work in front of consumers.

Then, in 2007, the iPhone appeared. Games were much easier to develop and easier to distribute through Apple's app store. Instead of just passing their work around to one another on blogs, independent game designers suddenly had a way to reach everyone — not just hard-core gamers, but their mothers, their mailmen and their college professors. Consumers who never would have put a quarter into an arcade or even set eyes on an Xbox 360 were now carrying a sophisticated game console with them, all the time, in their pockets or their purses.

This had a profound impact on game design. In the era of consoles, most games were designed to come to life on a stationary piece of furniture — a television or a desktop computer. The games were built accordingly, around long narratives (quests, wars, the rise and fall of civilizations) that could be explored comfortably while sitting cross-legged on a living-room carpet.

Smartphone games are built on a very different model. The iPhone's screen is roughly the size of a playing card; it responds not to the fast-twitch button combos of a controller but to more intuitive and intimate motions: poking, pinching, tapping, tickling. This has encouraged a very different kind of game: Tetris-like little puzzles, broken into discrete bits, designed to be played anywhere, in any context, without a manual, by any level of player. (Charles Pratt, a researcher in New York University's Game Center, refers to such games as "knitting games.") You could argue that these are *pure* games: perfectly designed mini-systems engineered to take us directly to the core of gaming pleasure without the distraction of narrative. The Angry Birds creators like to compare their game with Super Mario Brothers. But the first and simplest level of Super Mario Brothers takes about a minute and a half to finish. The first level of Angry Birds takes around 10 seconds.

OF ALL THE stupid games I've played, I became addicted to only one: Drop7, a candy-colored fusion of Tetris and Sudoku. Like its ancestors, Drop7 is basically a miniature obsessive-compulsive-disorder playground. The computer tries to fill up the screen while you try to keep it empty. It took me a few days to figure out the game's basic strategies (pay attention to the gray discs) then a few more weeks to figure out some more advanced tricks (focus on the grid's edges), and before long I entered the danger zone. I was playing when I should have been doing dishes, bathing my children, conversing with relatives, reading the newspaper and especially (especially) writing. The game was an anesthetic, an escape pod, a snorkel, a Xanax, a dental hygienist with whom to exchange soothingly meaningless banter before going under the pneumatic drill of Life. Soon I found myself struggling in the net of real addiction. Even as I pressed "New Game," my brain would be thinking, very consciously, I have to stop playing this game. But I didn't. Instead, I spread the Drop7 virus to other people: my wife, my friends, my mother, my in-laws. I found myself playing in all kinds of extreme situations: at 3 a.m., during a severe gastrointestinal crisis; immediately after an intense discussion with my mother; shortly after learning that my dog — the warm, emoting mammal I lived with for 12 years — was probably dying of cancer.

I wanted to understand how such a little game had managed, in such a short time, to drill down and implant its eggs right in the core of my life. So I e-mailed Frank Lantz, the man who designed Drop7. Lantz co-founded a company called Area/Code, is the director of New York University's Game Center and is just generally one of New York City's reigning geniuses of the mysteries of games. (He once oversaw a physical version of Pac-Man, enacted by actual humans, on the grid of New York City streets.) His company had just been purchased by Zynga, one of the titans of stupid games. I wanted to ask him: What is the secret genius of stupid games? Why am I so susceptible to them? How did Drop7 manage to take over my brain? First, though, I asked him if he could help me in another way: if he happened to know of any young design geniuses who were working on the problem of stupid games — someone likely to invent the next Drop7 or Angry Birds or Bejeweled but who had yet to be absorbed by one of the big companies.

Lantz responded with an e-mail that contained, in its entirety, a single name: Zach Gage.

THE FIRST THING Zach Gage did, when I walked into his apartment, was apologize for the mess. He had just finished building, in a corner of his living room, an old-fashioned arcade cabinet — the kind of wooden, vending-machine-size techno-altar you would have seen teenagers huddled around in skating rinks in the early 1980s, except this one had a giant Mac monitor for its screen and a Mac mini for its guts and could play more than 3,000 games: everything from the paradigm-shifting superclassics (Space Invaders, Pac-Man) to experimental metagames that Gage and his indie-designer friends invented — with no budget, sometimes in just a few hours — over the last year or two.

Gage referred to his arcade as "a little shrine to games." Building it, he said, had been his summer project; it cost him around six weeks and $1,000. He ordered parts from Hong Kong, then stripped and cut something like 100 wires, then figured out software to map them all to the various buttons. He had to learn the differences between Japanese joysticks (precise, delicate, sensitive) and American (tough, in order to withstand the constant abuse of meaty, unskilled hands).

He did all this out of a sense of deep technological longing. Gage was born in 1985 — one year after Tetris was born in the Soviet Union — which means he grew up in the era of home-video-game systems like Super Nintendo and Xbox. As a game nerd, he wondered what the heyday of public arcades might have been like: all of those actual bodies sharing the same physical space in order to pour themselves, coin by coin, into digital worlds — a kind of protosocial-gaming. His arcade was an attempt to try to begin to understand that, and playing it had inspired some thoughts that surprised me coming out of the mouth of a 26-year-old who created his career largely online.

"Having just built this, I'm seeing how much I hate the Internet," Gage told me. "I mean, I really like the Internet and what it's done for games — it's been amazing. But in so many ways it's just terrible. Arcade cabinets did a lot of things that were really smart that we never gave them credit for. There's a lot of social psychology embedded in that structure." The Xbox, he explained, offered only a few games designed to be played along with other people in the same room. "No one is designing games like that anymore," he said. "It's very terrible."

Gage is an indie game designer — the Bon Iver to Rovio's Katy Perry, the artisanal free-range heirloom-turkey breeder to Zynga's factory farm. He works out of his apartment and has long hair and a perpetually in-progress beard. He works on games mostly by himself, collaborating occasionally with friends, and sometimes he drops into immersive research sessions that can last for weeks. One recent session was intended to figure out why people like playing word games, a genre Gage has always hated. (He thinks it's cheating to build a game on top of a system that already exists, like words or numbers.) So he spent two weeks playing Bookworm, Words With Friends and Wurdle, during which he decided that the genre suffered from a serious lack of strategy — aside from Scrabble, he says, most of those games are just dressed-up word searches.

The result of this was SpellTower, Gage's newest and most successful game, which allows users to create towers by building words from letters in adjacent boxes. In its first two months, he says, it earned him enough money to live off for two years.

Gage's journey into the world of stupid games started, like many people's, with Tetris. He watched his girlfriend playing it on her iPod one day and noticed the clumsiness of the game's touch-screen interface. Gage was horrified. (He can be hilariously indignant about what he sees as bad game design.)

"The iPhone has all these wonderful features, and no one was making use of them," he told me, sounding a little like Howard Roark in "The Fountainhead." "Everyone was trying to figure out a way to shoehorn games they'd already made onto the platform. Tetris wasn't built around a touch screen. If we hadn't had those original games, and we'd only had touch screens, you'd never see a game like that. It would never have come up naturally, because it's not good. So I started making a game to explore that, to try and figure out what multitouch Tetris would be like."

The result was a game called Unify, a kind of bidirectional Tetris in which colored blocks drift in from opposite edges of the screen and meet in the middle. The game is addictive; it seems determined to explore some previously neglected intersection in the brain of motor skills and our capacity to track multiple objects simultaneously. It was critically acclaimed but only a modest success, in terms of sales, though Gage didn't seem to mind. "Coming at it from an art background," he said, "my interest is solely in getting to play with some new technology that no one's solved. Unify is, as far as I know, the very first time that anyone's ever made a multitouch puzzle-block game."

Gage's parents are both artists, and he has an M.F.A. from Parsons in New York; he comes off as the classic young artist toiling away in his garret, except instead of anatomy books and turpentine and canvases, he's surrounded by board games and old controllers and Xbox discs. For several years, Gage scraped out a living from a combination of teaching gigs, speaking engagements and game sales — with game sales being the least reliable contributor. He seems basically unconcerned about money. In fact, one of Gage's current projects is a satire of the current state of the gaming industry, especially companies' tendency to try to cash in by copying the latest trend. The game's working title is "Unify Birds." It's exactly the same as Unify except that it has been redesigned in the most superficial possible way: Gage has turned all of the blocks into colorful, wide-eyed birds. "I made a couple of other little changes," Gage says, "but mainly I just made everything superadorable. It's been really interesting, because I've showed it to people who liked Unify, and they'll play it, and they'll be like: 'Oh, man, Zach. This is a really good game. This is better.' They wondered what I've changed."

Gage let me play Unify Birds. It felt, immediately, like a much better game — a game, in fact, that might even become a hit.

THERE ARE PEOPLE who see the proliferation of stupid games as a good thing. In fact, they believe that games may be the answer to all of humanity's problems. In her book "Reality Is Broken," Jane McGonigal argues that play is possibly the best, healthiest, most productive activity a human can undertake — a gateway to our ideal psychological state. Games aren't an escape from reality, McGonigal contends, they are an optimal form of engaging it. In fact, if we could just find a way to impose game mechanics on top of everyday life, humans would be infinitely better off. We might even use these approaches to help solve real-world problems like obesity, education and government abuse. Some proponents point to successful examples of games applied to everyday life: Weight Watchers and frequent-flier miles, for example.

Corporations, of course, have been using similar strategies for decades, hooking consumers on products by giving them constant small victories for spending money (think of the old Monopoly game promotion at McDonald's). The buzzword for this is "gamification" and the ubiquity of computers and smartphones has only supercharged these tendencies. Gartner, a technology research firm, predicted last year that, in the near future, "a gamified service for consumer-goods marketing and customer retention will become as important as Facebook, eBay or Amazon." Companies have already used online games to sneakily advertise sugary cereals directly to children.

Although there is a certain utopian appeal to McGonigal's "games for change" model, I worry about the dystopic potential of gamification. Instead of just bombarding us with jingles, corporations will be able to inject their messages directly into our minds with ads disguised as games. Gamification seeks to turn the world into one giant chore chart covered with achievement stickers — the kind of thing parents design for their children — though it raises the potentially terrifying question of who the parents are. This, I fear, is the dystopian future of stupid games: amoral corporations hiring teams of behavioral psychologists to laser-target our addiction cycles for profit.

Mark Pincus, founder and chief executive of Zynga, said recently that game mechanics "will be the most valuable skill in the new economy." He should know. His game FarmVille, a farm simulator that dominated Facebook in 2009, is one of the most successful and controversial stupid games of all time. (The game's usage peaked, in early

2010, at nearly 85 million players.) FarmVille became notorious, especially in its early days, for its expansionist zeal: the way it used the architecture of Facebook to make itself go viral, autoposting constant status updates on its users' walls. The game is free but constantly nudges its players toward spending money and recruiting their friends.

By early 2010, millions of people had joined anti-Zynga Facebook pages. Facebook eventually cracked down on some of these more extreme practices. Zynga has now expanded its focus to include mobile phones. (Last month, Zynga introduced its own independent platform, Zynga.com.) As the economy of the actual world tanked, Zynga's virtual economies grew and grew, generating a real-world fortune. In 2010, the company reportedly had a $400 million profit. As of summer, when Zynga celebrated its third birthday, the company had studios in Beijing, Tokyo, Dallas, Boston, Baltimore, Bangalore, Los Angeles, Dublin and New York. During one particularly active stretch, it was buying another game company every month. It reportedly even tried to buy Rovio, the creator of Angry Birds, for $2.25 billion. (Rovio declined.)

Zynga's most popular game, Draw Something, has around 14 million daily players. Through its sheer size and scale, the company seems to be pushing the iPhone-game economy toward something like the old Triple-A model. One of its more recent games, Empires and Allies, was introduced in 12 countries simultaneously and attracted 10 million players in 10 days.

Some people argue that Zynga's signature games — FarmVille, FishVille — shouldn't even be called games. As Nicholas Carlson of the Web site Business Insider wrote: "They are click-machines powered by the human need to achieve progress by a predictable path and a willingness to pay small amounts of money to make that progress go faster. They are not 'games.' " But you could argue that games like FarmVille are in fact just the logical end of gamification: gamified games. They have the appearance of games, they inspire the compulsions of games, but for many people they are not fun like games.

Which brings us back to my addiction to Drop7.

When I spoke to Frank Lantz, the creator of Drop7, he seemed humbled by his own game. He said Drop7 felt less like something that he and his team had created than something they had discovered — "a little corner of the universe that people hadn't visited before, that predates us and will be around after we're gone." He's not sure why the game is so addictive, just that it is. (He said he even found himself enjoying it when he was play-testing, which is usually a purely analytical process.) Lantz's best explanation is that Drop7 occupies a "hinge in the universe" that is at once mathematical (it allows you to play between the ordinal and cardinal meanings of a number) and spiritual: it holds you in a place between conscious problem-solving and pure intoxication. Which, come to think of it, is probably the cognitive signature of all the great stupid games.

Lantz seemed undisturbed by the dark side of stupid games, like addiction or cynical corporate hijacking. He said that real games are far too fragile and complex to be engineered by corporations and that their appeal goes much deeper than reward schedules. "It's as hard to make a really good game as it is to make a really good movie or opera or hat," he told me. "Sure, there's mathematics to it, but it's also a piece of culture. The type of game you play is also a part of how you think about yourself as a person. There's no formula that's going to solve that equation. It's impossible, because it's infinitely deep and wonderful."

As for my nightmare vision of a world splintered by addiction to stupid games, Lantz had a different perspective. He said that he liked to think Drop7 was not only addictive but also, on some level, about addiction. Games, he told me, are like "homebrew neuroscience" — "a little digital drug you can use to run experiments on your own brain." Part of the point of letting them seduce you, as Lantz sees it, is to come out the other side a more interesting and self-aware person; more conscious of your habits, weaknesses, desires and strengths. "It's like heroin that is abstracted or compressed or stylized," he said. "It gives you a window into your brain that doesn't crush your brain."

I tried to think about what — if anything — I had learned from this window into my brain. Like their spiritual forefather, Tetris, most stupid games are about walls: building them, scaling them, knocking them down. Walls made of numbers, walls made of digital bricks, walls with green pigs hiding behind them. They're like miniature boot camps of containment. Ultimately, I realized, these games are also about a more subtle and mysterious form of wall-building: the internal walls we build to compartmentalize our time, our attention, our lives. The legendary game designer Sid Meier once defined a game as, simply, "a series of interesting choices." Maybe that's the secret genius of stupid games: they force us to make a series of interesting choices about what matters, moment to moment, in our lives.

Lantz told me that the deepest relationship he has ever had with a game was with poker, to which he was almost dangerously addicted. "Somehow teetering on the edge was part of the fun for me," he said. "It was like a tightrope walk between this transcendently beautiful and cerebral thing that gave you all kinds of opportunities to improve yourself — through study and self-discipline, making your mind stronger like a muscle — and at the same time it was pure self-destruction. There's no word for that in English, for a thing that does both of those at the same time. But it's wonderful."

I asked him if he knew a word for that in another language.

He said no, but then he thought for a minute.

"I think it's 'game,' " he said. "I think the word for that is 'game.' "

SAM ANDERSON is the magazine's critic at large. He last wrote about Dickens World, a theme park in England.

When Fantasy Football Becomes an Addiction

BLOG | BY C.D. CARTER | NOV. 27, 2012

I'VE PLAYED FANTASY FOOTBALL since 2006, when I was a 22-year-old cub reporter at The Gazette in Prince George's County, Md., and the paper's sports editor asked me to fill in the last spot in the office's fantasy league. I thought it silly, and that I'd be a natural at the game. After all, I had watched 12 hours of football with my dad every Sunday since I was 10 years old. I knew which players were good. I knew which players weren't. What else was there to know?

Now, at 29, I cannot watch football the way it was meant to be watched. I watch for stats. I fret about fantasy points, not game outcomes. The game, in short, is meaningless.

I don't watch playoff games. I don't care who wins the Super Bowl. I have loyalty to no one but myself and my pretend roster of random players from across the league. I can't recall the agony of emotional investment in a real team — the ability to feel that joy and pain has long left me, crowded out by fantasy obsession.

There is no joy, only anxiety, only pain, only disappointment. When I win a fantasy game, I'm only happy not to lose. When I lose, I'm crushed.

On Twitter, I found hundreds just like me: awash in the statistical minutia of a game that challenges its players to compose a lineup that will score more fake points than their opponents' fake players, willing to put in any amount of research to find an advantage over their opponents.

I was immersed — I am immersed — in the roiling, everlasting Twitter chatter that is today's fantasy football arena, where ideas are championed and derided and parroted and contradicted every minute of every day by wise and stupid alike. Twitter, for fantasy fiends, is an echo chamber and battleground, all at once.

ANN JOHANSSON FOR THE NEW YORK TIMES

The control room of the NFL Network's RedZone channel, which reduces football to a real-time highlight reel of scores.

Some of these obsessives make a living from the fantasy football knowledge they've contributed to the growing industry. I'm in occasional contact with these purveyors of fantasy groupthink and innovation, as I have a side gig as a writer for The Fake Football (as well as with NFL Jerks), run by guys with equal fantasy fervor.

Some addicts, like me, are left to answer questions from curious fantasy owners and hope for the occasional retweet from a fantasy bigwig as we fight for the attention of 32 million fantasy football owners, according to estimates from the Fantasy Sports Trade Association.

Of all the daily constructive exchanges, petty spats and frenetic 140-character volleys among Twitter's fantasy freaks, the issue of obsession — addiction — is rarely broached. It goes unacknowledged, I think, because in a dank flophouse, junkies don't ponder the ill effects of their addictions. They just do their drugs. They get high.

Kimberly Young, a licensed psychologist and founder of the Center of Internet Addiction, told me fantasy sports addiction is hardly different from other Web-based vices. Many online addictions, Young said, stem from a desperate need to control an outcome — any outcome.

"It's just an illusion of control, of course, but that's the driving force," Young, a psychology professor at St. Bonaventure University, told me.

She said most patients who come to her asking for help with their insatiable need to research pigskin stats at every hour of the day are men in their 20s. No surprise there — 80 percent of fantasy footballers are men. Almost every fantasy addict has an alternative to Young's prescription of total Internet detox.

"When I tell them there's an abstinence component, they tell me they'll just cut back," she said. "But they can't cut back. It's an all-consuming activity for them, but many think they can have just that one cigarette. It doesn't work like that."

I was surprised, after hearing Young's tales of life-destroying cases of fantasy sports addiction, to learn that Internet addiction hasn't made the cut as an official disorder in psychology's universe of definable problems.

The literature, as outlined in "Abnormal Psychology," defines Internet addiction as an impulse control condition that, if left unchecked, alters an addict's neurotransmitters in their brain while they engage their vice. Changing neurotransmitters — I can almost feel this happen when I scour the waiver wire, exploring every last statistical crevice for the player who will bring me victory that week — creates altered psychological states that bring euphoria to an addict's ravaged brain.

Enough of this euphoria, like with gambling or drinking or drugs, brings an Internet addict back to the glowing screen for more. I can attest: Devouring fantasy football tidbits, no matter how meaningless or numerically abstract, makes me happy. I think it makes me happy, anyhow.

I told Young that I was a fantasy football addict, but like any addict — even one who has admitted his problem — I was no fan of the solution.

David Devaney, who lives in Baltimore and works in sales, said his fantasy addiction peaked a few years back during a drive through the mountains of western Massachusetts on the way to visit family.

With his wife and daughter in tow, Devaney pulled over before they traversed the highest parts of the mountainous drive, where he knew he'd lose all phone and Internet connection. Devaney had forgotten to plug in a last-minute waiver wire pickup, and game time was 10 short minutes away. An empty roster spot, for any fantasy addict, is a mortal sin, and enough to make you sick.

"I'm up there, basically climbing these huge rocks, doing anything I can to get one bar on my phone, any sort of connection," he said. "I'm essentially fully extending my arm in the air and I'm setting my lineup, and I just stopped and thought, 'It's ridiculous that I'm doing this.' "

As an addict, as someone who has gone to humiliating lengths to tweak a lineup at the last minute, I had to ask: Was it worth it?

“No,” Devaney said flatly. “I did all that for some guy who got me five points that day.”

It was during the 2010 season that Devaney’s fantasy obsession had chipped away at his undying love for the Philadelphia Eagles. He said secretly rooting for various Dallas Cowboys on his fantasy squad — specifically, the reviled Miles Austin — and the New England rock-climbing, bar-searching incident were his rock bottom, the point at which he knew he had to remove fantasy football like a tumor.

“I was getting so lost in it,” he said, recalling hours spent in the glow of a laptop, analyzing waiver wire players and trade offers until they were indecipherable. “Everything revolved around maximizing points. It was consuming me. I wasn’t thinking about the game of football when I’d sit down to watch football. I was thinking about the players. Things got bad.”

So Devaney quit, just like that. He turned down offers from friends and coworkers who had for years bashed heads with Devaney in fake football matchups. The temptation was there, to join just one league, to do just one little draft, Devaney said, but he turned down every offer. The 2011 season started with Devaney planted on his couch, caring for nothing but his beloved Eagles.

“I tell everyone I know how great it is,” he told me over the phone. I dreaded what came next, what I knew he’d tell me, because he knows me, because he was me. “I highly suggest it to you. Just quit. It’s freeing. You won’t even miss it. I promise.”

I laughed as politely as possible.

“Seriously,” Devaney said, “it’ll make you feel older, more mature.”

I told him I’d consider it, the easy lie of an addict.

Austin Lee, when he’s not working in California’s movie industry, is writing in-depth fantasy analyses for Pro Football Focus, a daily resource to any hardcore fantasy footballer. He knows what it’s like to be trapped in the vortex of fantasy football Twitter chatter. You read a couple of dozen tweets from industry authorities and casual fans, you read a few more, you click links that lead to more links that lead to more links, and what started as a quick check of the Twitter feed turns into a two-hour orgy of stats and comparisons and player comparables. Tumbling down the rabbit hole of endless information is a terribly easy pastime.

Lee repeated a common refrain from my pool of justification when he said, "I thought I could keep it under control."

"But when all social contributions with friends and family were fantasy football related," he said, "that was an indicator that I needed to unplug."

Fantasy addiction, like anything that consumes hours and thoughts with equal ferocity, takes a physical toll on obsessives. I know, when my head hits the pillow on Sunday night, that sleep will be fleeting, even if I manage to banish thoughts of fake football long enough to fall asleep.

"I was losing a lot of sleep over waiver wire moves and trades and other decisions," Lee said. "It had a lot of weight to it, a lot of meaning. You just lie there awake and you think, I know I can find the right fit, I can come up with the right combination. I just need to try harder."

Lee's wife is an avid fantasy footballer, too, but even she grew weary of her husband's endless machinations — his trade offers, his fretting over whom to start and whom to sit.

"I knew then that I had crossed a bad threshold," he said.

Lee cut back, but found that the growth of fantasy made it impossible for any football fan to give it the cold shoulder.

"If you're a real addict, you have lots of people who can make your obsession seem completely normal," he said. "If you need that kind of confirmation, lots of people are there to tell you it's O.K., because they're addicted, too."

Melissa Jacobs remembers fantasy football when it was by geeks, for geeks, of geeks. Jacobs, a San Francisco native and former ESPN producer who founded the site TheFootballGirl.com and has 5,220 faithful Twitter followers who digest her weekly fantasy wisdom nuggets, played fantasy when it was a subculture, way before ESPN dedicated an entire hour of Sunday morning program to people's make-believe football roster decisions.

In the '90s, when fantasy scores were tallied from real life ink printed on real life newspaper every Monday and Tuesday morning, there was no massive online community of fantasy obsessives. There was you and your league members.

"I was playing it when it was totally socially taboo," said Jacobs, who now lives in Washington. "I was very closeted — we all were. It was considered a very dorky pastime — it was seen as sort of a freakish hobby. I'm not so sure people today realize that. No one is embarrassed about it anymore."

Lineup decisions still churned, she said, but the infrastructure of fantasy sports addiction — namely, the Internet — did not exist in any mainstream way.

"Trust me," Jacobs said, "I wanted to talk to someone about it. But no one played, so I kept it to myself."

Twitter isn't the lone feeder of my fantasy addiction. There's also the RedZone Channel, which caters to fantasy players by only showing games in which teams are on the cusp of scoring, usually inside the opponent's 20-yard line. RedZone reduces football to a real-time highlight reel of scores. The channel, in short, is a fantasy addict's most precious gift and most threatening enabler.

Watching RedZone, especially during a flurry of Sunday afternoon scoring, has become an experiment in how much stress my heart can handle without failing. I'm not proud to admit that, when I watch football alone in my basement, I don't shut the bathroom door when nature calls. I leave it open enough to see half my giant TV screen. On the rare Sunday when I have company in the basement, I close the door and feel the beginnings of an anxiety attack constrict my breathing. I have to see what's happening, what my guys are doing.

Watching the cavalcade of football games as they unfold won't change anything. Unlike a tree falling in the woods with no one around, your No. 3 wide receiver is going to fetch you three lousy fantasy points, whether you watch every snap or none at all. This realization, in the frenzy of Sunday football, means nothing.

"You can see the terrible impact of being an alcoholic right away," Lee said, recalling his darkest fantasy days. "But this consumes your thoughts. It really eats away at you."

It forces you to watch the RedZone Channel from the comfort of a toilet.

Chris Wesseling is a senior N.F.L. editor at Rotoworld, an online treasure trove of fantasy goodness that I peruse with great interest every day, many times a day. Wesseling has taken on a godfather-type role in the fantasy community — a sober voice of reasonable advice, never brash or cocky, like so many self-professed fantasy football experts who dispatch a thousand grating tweets a day. Wesseling will tell you what to do without telling you what to do. In short, I strive to be like him.

The culture of fantasy football has gone to a progressively darker place since Wesseling started playing the game in the mid-1990s. There is hardly any acknowledgement, he said, that this is a game for nerds.

"There should be just a bit of shame involved," he told me. "That gets left behind as the popularity rages out of control. Let's face it, there's not much separating fantasy football from Dungeons and Dragons. You're living out a fantasy through the actions of someone else. Teddy Roosevelt would be appalled at such behavior. Nobody cares about your fantasy team except you."

Wesseling said he has liberally employed Twitter's block button as a preemptive weapon against fantasy owners looking to publicly embarrass fantasy's most respected voices.

"My track record on fantasy advice speaks for itself, so of course I'm not going to take it well if one piece of advice in thousands is thrown back in my face because it didn't work out for that fantasy owner that week," he said. "The older I get, the less I'm willing to suffer fools gladly — particular fools complaining about a quality free service. Who raised these disrespectful animals, anyway?"

My wife is pregnant with our first child, a boy, due in late December. When the doctor announced the due date, I was filled with joy and terror and excitement. I hugged my wife, her pregnant belly exposed in the sterility of the doctor's office. For the ten thousandth time, I told my wife how much I loved her. We kissed.

Then came the thought, my addiction tapping me on the shoulder, reminding me of its omnipresence. Hello, it said, I'm still here, and I'm not going anywhere.

I tried to banish the thought, to vanquish it before it was fully formed, but I couldn't.

The last week of December, I thought — consumed by shame — is fantasy football championship week.

I want nothing more than to have a normal relationship with fantasy football, normal enough to one day share the game with my son when we're all making fantasy start-sit decisions on floating holograms in front of our eight-dimensional televisions hovering weightlessly before us.

I looked to Patrick Lane, a Maryland state trooper and my friend since middle school, for advice. How, I asked Lane one night during an instant message screaming match about the fantasy value of Ryan Mathews, can you go to bed on Monday night, just as your fantasy players have their last shots to notch a win for your make-believe football team?

"Mostly my thoughts are this: I'm tired and I would like to go to bed," said Lane, whom I introduced to fantasy a year after I took the plunge. He has often berated me for watching every minute of every prime-time game, and staying on Twitter until 2 a.m. discussing fantasy implications. "Watching games all day Sunday and then a late night game and then another on Monday? After a while, I've had enough. I'm not going to kill myself to watch one guy maybe not do anything. I'll find out in the morning."

Lane will wrench open his eyelids and watch the waning minutes of "Monday Night Football" if, and only if, his beloved Redskins are playing. He still sees the game through the eyes of a real fan. Good for him.

Fantasy obsessives who considered themselves full-fledged addicts told me, yes, it's easy to fall down the rabbit hole and go to that dark place where fantasy decisions matter more than anything. But, they said, an addict has to know when to unplug.

That isn't an option for true addicts. It isn't an option for me.

"Of course I can empathize with other people who are addicted," said J.J Zachariason, author of the book, "The Late Round Quarterback," a persuasive counterargument to fantasy dogma that says owners must draft elite quarterbacks to win championships. "But at the same time, I think like any addiction, you need to know when to stop. I guess that's counterintuitive, but I think it's always good when people realize a problem and seek help. I, and a lot of other fantasy people, know when and how to stop."

With parenthood comes perspective, right? Things that were once paramount become utterly meaningless; priorities change a hundred times until you can't remember what was so incredibly important about that hobby you used to hold dear. After a few years of parenthood, no one can even remember life before kids, right?

Having a baby, maybe, will be the stake driven through the heart of my fantasy football addiction. Part of me — most of me — hopes it is.

C.D. CARTER is a reporter, an author of zombie stories, and a writer for The Fake Football and NFL Jerks.

Video Games Aren't Addictive

OPINION | BY CHRISTOPHER J. FERGUSON AND PATRICK MARKEY | APRIL 1, 2017

IS VIDEO GAME addiction a real thing?

It's certainly common to hear parents complain that their children are "addicted" to video games. Some researchers even claim that these games are comparable to illegal drugs in terms of their influence on the brain — that they are "digital heroin" (the neuroscientist Peter C. Whybrow) or "digital pharmakeia" (the neuroscientist Andrew Doan). The American Psychiatric Association has identified internet gaming disorder as a possible psychiatric illness, and the World Health Organization has proposed including "gaming disorder" in its catalog of mental diseases, along with drug and alcohol addiction.

This is all terribly misguided. Playing video games is not addictive in any meaningful sense. It is normal behavior that, while perhaps in many cases a waste of time, is not damaging or disruptive of lives in the way drug or alcohol use can be.

Let's start with the neuroscientific analogy: that the areas in the brain associated with the pleasures of drug use are the same as those associated with the pleasures of playing video games. This is true but not illuminating. These areas of the brain — those that produce and respond to the neurotransmitter dopamine — are involved in just about any pleasurable activity: having sex, enjoying a nice conversation, eating good food, reading a book, using methamphetamines.

The amount of dopamine involved in these activities, however, differs widely. Playing a video game or watching an amusing video on the internet causes roughly about as much dopamine to be released in your brain as eating a slice of pizza. By contrast, using a drug like methamphetamine can cause a level of dopamine release 10 times that or more. On its own, the fact that a pleasurable activity involves dopamine release tells us nothing else about it.

BRANDON CELI

A large-scale study of internet-based games recently published in the American Journal of Psychiatry bears out our skepticism about this "addiction." Using the American Psychiatric Association's own metrics for ascertaining psychiatric disorder, the study's researchers found that at most 1 percent of video game players *might* exhibit characteristics of an addiction and that the games were significantly less addictive than, say, gambling.

More damning, the study found that almost none of those classified as being possibly addicted to video games experienced negative outcomes from this addiction. That is, the mental, physical and social health of these potential "addicts" was not different from that of individuals who were not addicted to video games. This suggests that the diagnosis of addiction doesn't make much sense to begin with.

Indeed, the biggest difference between addicts and non-addicts that the study found was that the addicts *played more video games.* This is a diagnosis that verges on mere tautology.

The risk here, of course, is that by treating the immoderate playing of video games as an addiction, we are pathologizing relatively normal behavior. Consider a common diagnostic question used to help identify addiction, such as "I always use X to relax after a bad day." Well, if X is methamphetamine, that's a worrisome choice, one that presumably indicates addiction. But if X is playing video games, how is that different from unwinding after work by knitting, watching sports or playing bridge?

We don't deny that new technologies come with some perils. We understand the nostalgia for the halcyon days of, say, the 1950s, when people were not yet bound to their personal technology and were free to enjoy the simpler pleasures of life, like stickball and climbing trees — and getting polio and having to wait in line at the bank to check your account balance.

We doubt most people would actually want to return to the good old days. We and our children are "addicted" to new technologies because, for the most part, they improve our lives or are simply pleasurable.

Evidence for addiction to video games is virtually nonexistent. That's not to say we and our children don't need to balance technology use with exercise, proper sleep and the responsibilities we have in real life. But indulging in panic about technology or nostalgia for a better past that never really existed does us no good.

CHRISTOPHER J. FERGUSON, a professor of psychology at Stetson University, and **PATRICK MARKEY**, a professor of psychology at Villanova, are the authors of "Moral Combat: Why the War on Video Games Is Wrong."

Early Facebook and Google Employees Form Coalition to Fight What They Built

BY NELLIE BOWLES | FEB. 4, 2018

SAN FRANCISCO — A group of Silicon Valley technologists who were early employees at Facebook and Google, alarmed over the ill effects of social networks and smartphones, are banding together to challenge the companies they helped build.

The cohort is creating a union of concerned experts called the Center for Humane Technology. Along with the nonprofit media watchdog group Common Sense Media, it also plans an anti-tech addiction lobbying effort and an ad campaign at 55,000 public schools in the United States.

The campaign, titled The Truth About Tech, will be funded with $7 million from Common Sense and capital raised by the Center for Humane Technology. Common Sense also has $50 million in donated media and airtime from partners including Comcast and DirecTV. It will be aimed at educating students, parents and teachers about the dangers of technology, including the depression that can come from heavy use of social media.

"We were on the inside," said Tristan Harris, a former in-house ethicist at Google who is heading the new group. "We know what the companies measure. We know how they talk, and we know how the engineering works."

The effect of technology, especially on younger minds, has become hotly debated in recent months. In January, two big Wall Street investors asked Apple to study the health effects of its products and to make it easier to limit children's use of iPhones and iPads. Pediatric and mental health experts called on Facebook last week to abandon a messaging service the company had introduced for children as young as 6.

PETER PRATO FOR THE NEW YORK TIMES

Jim Steyer, left, and Tristan Harris in Common Sense's headquarters. Common Sense is helping fund the The Truth About Tech campaign.

Parenting groups have also sounded the alarm about YouTube Kids, a product aimed at children that sometimes features disturbing content.

"The largest supercomputers in the world are inside of two companies — Google and Facebook — and where are we pointing them?" Mr. Harris said. "We're pointing them at people's brains, at children."

Silicon Valley executives for years positioned their companies as tight-knit families and rarely spoke publicly against one another. That has changed. Chamath Palihapitiya, a venture capitalist who was an early employee at Facebook, said in November that the social network was "ripping apart the social fabric of how society works."

The new Center for Humane Technology includes an unprecedented alliance of former employees of some of today's biggest tech companies. Apart from Mr. Harris, the center includes Sandy

Parakilas, a former Facebook operations manager; Lynn Fox, a former Apple and Google communications executive; Dave Morin, a former Facebook executive; Justin Rosenstein, who created Facebook's Like button and is a co-founder of Asana; Roger McNamee, an early investor in Facebook; and Renée DiResta, a technologist who studies bots.

The group expects its numbers to grow. Its first project to reform the industry will be to introduce a Ledger of Harms — a website aimed at guiding rank-and-file engineers who are concerned about what they are being asked to build. The site will include data on the health effects of different technologies and ways to make products that are healthier.

Jim Steyer, chief executive and founder of Common Sense, said the Truth About Tech campaign was modeled on antismoking drives and focused on children because of their vulnerability. That may sway tech chief executives to change, he said. Already, Apple's chief executive, Timothy D. Cook, told The Guardian last month that he would not let his nephew on social media, while the Facebook investor Sean Parker also recently said of the social network that "God only knows what it's doing to our children's brains."

Mr. Steyer said, "You see a degree of hypocrisy with all these guys in Silicon Valley."

The new group also plans to begin lobbying for laws to curtail the power of big tech companies. It will initially focus on two pieces of legislation: a bill being introduced by Senator Edward J. Markey, Democrat of Massachusetts, that would commission research on technology's impact on children's health, and a bill in California by State Senator Bob Hertzberg, a Democrat, which would prohibit the use of digital bots without identification.

Mr. McNamee said he had joined the Center for Humane Technology because he was horrified by what he had helped enable as an early Facebook investor.

“Facebook appeals to your lizard brain — primarily fear and anger,” he said. “And with smartphones, they’ve got you for every waking moment.”

He said the people who made these products could stop them before they did more harm.

“This is an opportunity for me to correct a wrong,” Mr. McNamee said.

How Social Media Gives Women a Voice

BY CLAIRE CAIN MILLER | FEB 9, 2018

SUSAN FOWLER HAD tried going to human resources. She had tried going to her managers. She had tried transferring departments. But nothing changed. The sexual and sexist comments she received as an engineer at Uber kept coming.

So she went online and wrote a 3,000-word blog post exposing the behavior.

A year later, a raft of executives, including Travis Kalanick, Uber's co-founder and chief executive, are gone. Ms. Fowler, meanwhile, has a new job, a book contract and a movie deal.

This has been a period when the whisper network moved online and became a shout. Suddenly, in a way they never had before, women have a voice, people are listening, and men are paying consequences.

It's happening now for a lot of reasons, but one of them is that social media has given victims a platform, a network of allies and a public presence that can't as easily be silenced. Social media, for all its flaws, has served as a democratizing force.

On Twitter, people in Hollywood described abuse. In Silicon Valley, a venture capitalist was fired after an accusatory Facebook post. With the #MeToo hashtag, a chorus of voices shared experiences of harassment and assault by famous men and, in much larger numbers, men who are not.

"Social media changed it dramatically," Tarana Burke said, talking about the #MeToo movement, which she started in 2006 and which went viral last year. "The internet is a great equalizer. The hashtag created a global community of support. That was a beautiful thing to watch."

The balance of power had long been tilted in the direction of men. They were the ones with the status and money to harass and abuse women, and then threaten, bribe or fire them if they complained. Only

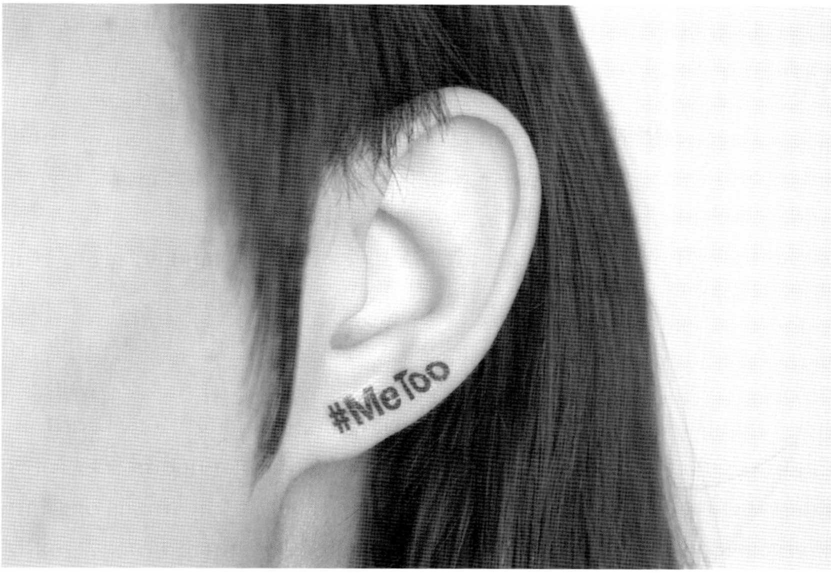

JOHN YUYI

about a quarter of women who have suffered harassment report it, and the main reasons that more don't are that they (rightly) fear retaliation, don't think anyone will do anything about it and don't want to face those consequences alone.

Social media changed much of that. It's harder to retaliate or ignore reports when the public is watching, or dismiss women's accusations when they are immediately bolstered by the stories of many more women.

Gretchen Carlson, the former Fox anchor who helped start the national reckoning, said in a recent interview at TEDWomen, "Social media has really helped us in this whole effort because it's given women the power to know they're not alone."

The medium can also be abused, spreading false allegations just as quickly. But if anything, that can be seen as a testament to the power women now hold.

Even the Tech Elite Are Worrying About Tech Addiction

BY FARHAD MANJOO | FEB. 9, 2018

YOUR PHONE BUZZES. A message, an Instagram post, a tweet — some bit of digital effluvia has come in, and it's right there, promising a brief but necessary hit of connection. All you have to do is look.

But, just as an experiment, how long can you resist looking? A minute? Two? If you make it that long, how do you start to feel? Can you concentrate? Does your mind wander at what you're missing? And if you give in — as you surely will, as you probably do many times a day — how do you feel about yourself?

The issue of "tech addiction" has been a staple of tabloidy panics for as long as anyone can remember. Yet this ancient worry has now taken on a new and more righteous flavor.

What is interesting is who has been pushing the issue. Several former Facebook executives, the very people who set up the Like-based systems of digital addiction and manipulation that now rule much of online life, have begun to speak out in alarm about our slavishness to digital devices.

And their worries seem resonant. Now that we all have phones, and we're all looking at them all the time, how can we deny that they hold some otherworldly, possibly unhealthy bondage over our brains?

"It's a social-validation feedback loop," Sean Parker, Facebook's first president, told Axios in an interview in November. He described Facebook and other social apps in terms once reserved for cigarettes — as products specifically engineered to exploit addiction pathways in human psychology. "God only knows what it's doing to our children's brains."

Others have echoed his sentiment.

"The short-term, dopamine-driven feedback loops we've created are destroying how society works," Chamath Palihapitiya, who once led

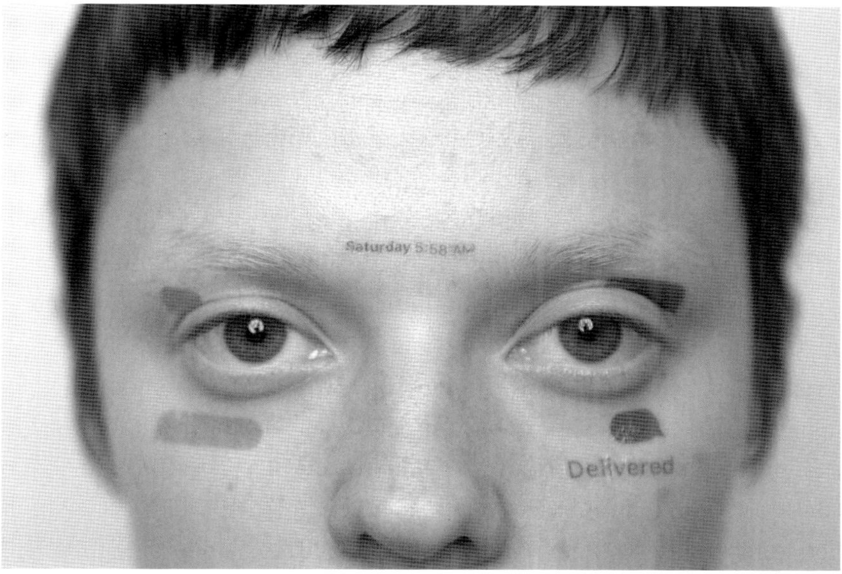

JOHN YUYI

Facebook's efforts at global growth and is now a venture capitalist, told an audience at Stanford's Graduate School of Business in December. The Guardian, meanwhile, found a handful of former Facebookers who said they would quit using social media for fear of being programmed by the social giant.

Even Wall Street has weighed in, with two large investors asking Apple in January to study the health effects of its products and to make it easier for parents to limit their children's use of iPhones and iPads.

Whether these Cassandras are correct is still a matter of scientific inquiry, though several studies suggest our phones do exert an addictive pull.

A study published in June by researchers at the University of Texas asked subjects to take a series of tests that required full cognitive attention. The researchers found that people who had their smartphones nearby — even though they were on silent — performed significantly worse than those whose phones were in another room. In other words, if your phone is nearby, you can never really stop thinking about it.

The bigger problem is what to do about any of this. Few laws or regulations prevent apps from keeping us hooked, and the tech industry has no serious ethical prohibitions against tinkering with software to drive engagement; indeed, at many tech companies, keeping people glued to the screen is the whole ballgame.

Sure, it's nice that the guys who created this machine are suddenly aware of its dangers. But other than stop our phones entirely — or pursuing some self-directed regimen of conscientious withdrawal, good luck with that! — we might truly be hosed.

Me and My Numb Thumb: A Tale of Tech, Texts and Tendons

COLUMN | BY NELLIE BOWLES | MAY 19, 2018

SAN FRANCISCO — It took me a few months to accept that I had given myself tendinosis in my phone thumb.

It is a depressingly modern condition in which the tendons around the thumb inflame as a result of repetitive strain — in my case because I had, for hours a day over years of a life, tapped that right-hand digit onto the glass of my smartphone.

The condition sounds like the subject of a local television news trend story about teenagers whose thumbs seize up while they play video games. It was definitely not something I, a mature professional, should ever have. I began to call it my numb thumb.

I had tried to prevent it, using other fingers on my phone when I felt early signs of pain. But they typed too slowly, so I stuck with my thumb, pressing it down to unlock the screen, and then using it to jab out texts and emails.

Eventually, my right thumb just stopped working. It could not muster the strength to press down on my phone. It was both numb and achy. And the pain that had started in my hand was now shooting down my arm. I had a problem, one I later learned was becoming common.

Suddenly, friends and co-workers all seemed to have similar stories about their thumbs, plus wrist braces I could borrow. And experts told me that although there is plenty of discussion about how teenagers are addicted to technology, adults are actually hit the hardest.

My doctor, who had me make a painful fist, said that I might have something called De Quervain's Tendinosis, which affects tendons on the thumb side of the wrist and is caused by chronic overuse of those tendons. He admonished me about tech addiction and about how if I continued this way, I would need surgery.

He sent me for acupuncture, which I had never tried before.

KIMBERLY SALT

"It's a crisis," said Sanjeev Kakar, an orthopedic surgeon at the Mayo Clinic in Minnesota who specializes in hand injuries and has seen an increase in the number of thumb "overuse cases." Dr. Kakar said he had noticed that the condition was spreading among adults and older people in particular.

"Your joints are a little stiffer," he told me. "Your tendons aren't as pliable as they used to be."

He added that numbness could be an early sign of carpal tunnel syndrome or, perhaps, nerve compression that is typically associated with competitive bowling.

Do I bowl? I do not bowl.

I called it numb, but it was also very painful, I told Dr. Kakar. He seemed relieved. The best cure, he said, was to stop using the thumb for a while.

"Change your texting behavior," he said. That sounds logical and easy — until you try to email left-handed.

Adults with tech-related injuries often refuse to admit they have a problem until injuries and addictive behavior progress to an extreme, said Nancy Ann Cheever, a professor of communications at California State University, Dominguez Hills, who studies technology and addiction.

"We assume teenagers are using their phones more, but it's actually not the case, because younger people tend to have a lot more awareness of their smartphone use," she said. "They have a more complete understanding of the harmful effects of smartphone use because they've been taught about it since they were kids."

Dr. Cheever has just completed a study of how anxious people get when they hear their phones receiving texts that they have been told not to answer. She measured their heart rates and how much they sweat.

"Very stressed," she said, summarizing the preliminary results.

When I recently walked into the office of Michelle Kuroda, a San Francisco acupuncturist, she said I was one of the lucky ones. She had just had two patients whose phone hands hurt so much that they had had to take leaves of absence from work.

"They were dropping things," Ms. Kuroda said. "They couldn't eat with forks."

She said that it was unnatural to concentrate so much movement in one digit on such a small flat surface.

"We're not meant to just use our thumbs all the time," she said. "We're meant to use all our fingers. That's what our grip is for."

She said the reason some people get phone thumb and others do not often comes down to stress. Cortisol and adrenaline, which the body releases when it feels stress, make one prone to inflammation and contribute to conditions like the one I was experiencing. She asked if I felt stressed, and I described a typical day monitoring Twitter.

"You kind of have a pre-existing condition just because of your lifestyle," she said.

Ms. Kuroda left me with a cluster of needles in my hand and arm and told me to do body scans for an hour. She also prescribed several antidotes. They included turmeric, an anti-inflammatory, and cannabidiol, a non-psychotropic marijuana plant extract more commonly known as CBD.

Panic over tech and addiction comes and goes. When a new study comes out with jarring numbers or a fancy new gadget hits the market, the flurry of stories and conversations will start anew. We tell ourselves the bigger issue must be among the teenagers. And quickly we all get over it.

After a few weeks of resting my right thumb, it felt a lot better and almost completely back to normal. I use my left hand now — quite a lot, in fact.

"Disruptions" is a weekly column exploring how technology is shaping our lives.

Facebook Unveils Redesign as It Tries to Move Past Privacy Scandals

BY MIKE ISAAC | APRIL 30, 2019

The social network rolled out a redesign, in the most visible signal of how it is starting to emphasize private communications.

MENLO PARK, CALIF. — Mark Zuckerberg declared in March that he planned to shift Facebook away from being a public town square and to private communications. Now, the chief executive is rolling out the first in a series of changes to achieve that.

On Tuesday at its annual developer conference, Facebook unveiled a redesign of its mobile app and desktop site. The revisions add new features to promote group-based communications instead of News Feed, where people publicly post a cascade of messages and status updates.

With the changes, users can more easily message one another and share news and other items with members of private groups on the site, the company said. Mr. Zuckerberg is working to integrate and encrypt Facebook's different messaging services, which include WhatsApp and Messenger. The company also plans to continue emphasizing its Stories product, which allows people to post updates that disappear after 24 hours. And it unveiled a spare, stark white look for Facebook, a departure from the site's largely blue-tinted design.

The features, when combined, "will end up creating a more trustworthy platform," Mr. Zuckerberg said in an interview. "Everywhere you can see and connect with friends, you'll be able to see and connect with groups; it's going to be woven into the fabric of Facebook."

The redesign is the most tangible sign of how the privacy scandals and user-data issues that have roiled Facebook are forcing change at the company. The social network has spent the past three years grappling with criticism that it did not properly protect its users' information, that it spread false news and other toxic content and that it was used as a tool for election interference. Last week, it said it expected to be fined up to $5 billion by the Federal Trade Commission for privacy violations, in what would be a record penalty against a technology company by the United States.

Facebook is also playing catch-up with people's shifting social media behavior. Questions about the benefits of social media and more recognition of its ills have prompted many to turn toward methods of private communications, such as messaging apps.

"By far, the three fastest-growing areas of online communication are private messaging, groups and Stories," Mr. Zuckerberg said. "In 2019, we expect the amount of Stories that are shared to outnumber the amount of Feed posts that are shared."

Eventually, he said, Facebook plans to roll out dozens of small product updates across its four main apps of WhatsApp, Instagram, Messenger and Facebook itself.

The shift raises questions for Facebook, including how it will make money from private communications. The company generates most of its $56 billion in annual revenue from targeted advertising that is based partly on what people publicly post about themselves.

"The challenge of steering the Facebook ship in this new, private direction is going to be massive," said Debra Aho Williamson, an internet analyst at eMarketer, a research firm. "And it leaves a lot of questions unaddressed, in particular how this shift will affect its equally massive advertising business."

Marc Rotenberg, president of the Electronic Privacy Information Center, said the changes were late given that privacy concerns "were raised many, many years ago" to Facebook.

The initial new features that were unveiled on Tuesday alter the site but do not amount to a full-scale overhaul. Facebook is adding a Groups tab to its main mobile app and desktop menus, for example. Recommendations for groups that users may want to join will pop up in various areas of the app. Messages meant for close friends and

JESSICA CHOU FOR THE NEW YORK TIMES

Mark Zuckerberg, the founder of Facebook, in Palo Alto, Calif., April 11, 2019.

family will have their own section inside Facebook Messenger. All in all, it will be hard for someone to open up Facebook and not see a prompt beckoning him or her to a group chat.

Facebook also revealed other changes. It plans to roll out its Dating feature to more than a dozen new countries, such as Thailand and Canada; the service is not available in the United States. Instagram introduced new digital shopping and commerce features inside the app.

And Facebook's Craigslist competitor, Marketplace, integrated shipping and payment capabilities for the first time. It allows people to pay for and ship items they have purchased from other Facebook users anywhere within the continental United States. Previously, users had to arrange payment privately, off Facebook.

The focus on Facebook Groups is convenient for the company because it reduces the amount of public content that it has to moderate and ultimately answer for, said Jennifer Grygiel, an assistant professor of media and communication at the Newhouse School at Syracuse University. "I think it's a way for them to offload responsibility," the professor said.

Facebook's developer conference, called F8, began in 2007 to entice developers to build apps for the social network. The company offered developers access to its so-called social graph, its rich web of user connections and personal data.

Last year, The New York Times and others revealed that Cambridge Analytica, a British political firm with developer access to Facebook's social graph, had harvested the personal information of millions of Facebook users without their consent, in order to build voter profiles for the Trump presidential campaign. That revelation brought heightened scrutiny to the social giant, particularly on how it handled users' information.

Facebook has since vowed to supervise its users' information more closely and placed greater restrictions on developer access. That makes this year's F8 more challenging for developers who have relied on the social network's data.

"It's going to make developing for the platform harder for a lot of these folks," Mr. Zuckerberg said. He added that any short-term difficulties for developers were worth the long-term benefit of greater user trust in the platform.

The new privacy direction may create other issues. Closed groups and encrypted services will make it more difficult to identify and root out dangerous or abusive behavior, Mr. Zuckerberg said, though he added that the company's automated systems had ways of detecting illicit activities — like examining traffic patterns — without scanning the content of private messages.

"There's still a lot more to do," he said, adding that the spotlight on the company had "definitely prompted more introspection around what direction our services should go in."

Glossary

attention deficit disorder A developmental condition that involves reduced attention span, hyperactivity and impulsiveness.

Blackberry A mobile smart device popular in the 2000s that was made obsolete by the introduction of smartphones.

coalition A group of individuals or organizations united to perform a certain activity.

cognitive behavioral therapy A form of psychological therapy designed to correct harmful thinking patterns.

cookies Messages stored in text files that communicate personal information to web pages.

cottage industries Individuals who perform labor out of their homes with equipment they own.

cyberbullying Cruel messages sent to a person through electronic means.

distracted driving Operating motor vehicles while texting or otherwise using smartphones.

dopamine A neurochemical associated with the brain's centers of movement and pleasure and reward.

encrypt To make secret.

ethics A philosophy of moral values.

euphoria A feeling of intense elation.

floppy disks A plastic disk designed to store computer data magnetically.

hacker A computer expert who breaks into computer networks for malicious reasons.

lockout technology Computer technology designed to prevent access.

monopoly A service controlled by one company.

multitask To do several tasks at once.

repetitive stress disorders Damage to tendons, muscles, nerves, joints or ligaments of the hand, arm and shoulders through repetitive movements.

Ritalin A drug prescribed to people suffering from attention deficit disorder.

sexting Sending nude or seminude photos to smartphones.

social engineering Manipulation of people that influences them to give up information they would normally kept secret.

venture capitalist An investor who provides funds to companies starting up with the expectation of profiting from the investment.

Media Literacy Terms

"Media literacy" refers to the ability to access, understand, critically assess and create media. The following terms are important components of media literacy, and they will help you critically engage with the articles in this title.

angle The aspect of a news story that a journalist focuses on and develops.

attribution The method by which a source is identified or by which facts and information are assigned to the person who provided them.

balance Principle of journalism that both perspectives of an argument should be presented in a fair way.

bias A disposition of prejudice in favor of a certain idea, person or perspective.

caption Identifying copy for a picture; also called a legend or cutline.

chronological order Method of writing a story presenting the details of the story in the order in which they occurred.

column A type of story that is a regular feature, often on a recurring topic, written by the same journalist, generally known as a columnist.

commentary A type of story that is an expression of opinion on recent events by a journalist generally known as a commentator.

credibility The quality of being trustworthy and believable, said of a journalistic source.

critical review A type of story that describes an event or work of art, such as a theater performance, film, concert, book, restaurant, radio or television program, exhibition or musical piece, and offers critical assessment of its quality and reception.

editorial Article of opinion or interpretation.

human interest story A type of story that focuses on individuals and how events or issues affect their life, generally offering a sense of relatability to the reader.

impartiality Principle of journalism that a story should not reflect a journalist's bias and should contain balance.

intention The motive or reason behind something, such as the publication of a news story.

interview story A type of story in which the facts are gathered primarily by interviewing another person or persons.

motive The reason behind something, such as the publication of a news story or a source's perspective on an issue.

op-ed An opinion piece that reflects a prominent individual's opinion on a topic of interest.

paraphrase The summary of an individual's words, with attribution, rather than a direct quotation of their exact words.

quotation The use of an individual's exact words indicated by the use of quotation marks and proper attribution.

reliability The quality of being dependable and accurate, said of a journalistic source.

rhetorical device Technique in writing intending to persuade the reader or communicate a message from a certain perspective.

source The origin of the information reported in journalism.

style A distinctive use of language in writing or speech; also a news or publishing organization's rules for consistent use of language with regard to spelling, punctuation, typography and capitalization, usually regimented by a house style guide.

tone A manner of expression in writing or speech.

Media Literacy Questions

1. Identify the various sources cited in the article "Computers: An Extra Becomes an Essential" (on page 10). How does Dirk Johnson attribute information to each of these sources in his article? How effective are Johnson's attributions in helping the reader identify his sources?

2. "In Korea, a Boot Camp Cure for Web Obsession" (on page 30) features several photographs. What do these photographs add to the article?

3. Compare the headlines of "Why We Can't Look Away From Our Screens" (on page 51) and "An Ugly Toll of Technology: Impatience and Forgetfulness" (on page 112). Which is a more compelling headline, and why? How could the less compelling headline be changed to better draw the reader's interest?

4. Do Daisuke Wakabayashi and Brian X. Chen demonstrate the journalistic principle of impartiality in their article "Google Says It Has Found Religion on Privacy" (on page 56)? If so, how did they do so? If not, what could they have included to make their article more impartial?

5. "Sext and the Single Girl" (on page 82) is a critical review. How does Cindi Leive balance her personal opinion with issues raised by the book? What is Leive's overall opinion of the book?

6. Does "Phone Makers Could Cut Off Drivers. So Why Don't They?" (on page 135) use multiple sources? What are the strengths of using multiple sources in a journalistic piece? What are the weaknesses?

7. Analyze the author's reporting in "Tech Backlash Grows as Investors Press Apple to Act on Children's Use" (on page 145). Do you think the content is balanced? What is the angle of this article?

8. "Your Kid's Phone Is Not Like a Cigarette" (on page 149) criticizes ad campaigns dealing with people's behavior with technology. Do you think this criticism is well-supported by Anya Kamenetz's arguments? Why or why not?

9. Identify each of the sources in "Parenting the Fortnite Addict" (on page 154) as a primary source or a secondary source. Evaluate the reliability and credibility of each source. How does your evaluation of each source change your perspective on this article?

10. "Just One More Game ..." (on page 166) covers different forms of Internet games. Look for author bias in the piece. Are you able to detect any? If so, identify possible reasons for this bias.

11. What is the style and tone of "How Social Media Gives Women a Voice" (on page 198)? How does this affect the purpose of the article? Why do you think this is?

12. What is the intention of the article "Me and My Numb Thumb: A Tale of Tech, Texts and Tendons" (on page 203)? How effectively does it achieve its intended purpose?

Citations

All citations in this list are formatted according to the Modern Language Association's (MLA) style guide.

BOOK CITATION

THE NEW YORK TIMES EDITORIAL STAFF. *Tech Addiction.* New York: New York Times Educational Publishing, 2020.

ONLINE ARTICLE CITATIONS

ANDERSON, SAM. "Just One More Game ..." *The New York Times*, 4 Apr. 2012, www.nytimes.com/2012/04/08/magazine/angry-birds-farmville-and-other-hyperaddictive-stupid-games.html.

BIERSDORFER, J. D. "A Hacker Tells All." *The New York Times*, 12 Aug. 2011, www.nytimes.com/2011/08/14/books/review/ghost-in-the-wires-by-kevin-mitnick-with-william-l-simon-book-review.html.

BILTON, NICK. "Disruptions: More Connected, Yet More Alone." *The New York Times*, 1 Sept. 2013, bits.blogs.nytimes.com/2013/09/01/disruptions-more-connected-yet-more-alone/.

BOWLES, NELLIE. "Early Facebook and Google Employees Form Coalition to Fight What They Built." *The New York Times*, 4 Feb. 2018, www.nytimes.com/2018/02/04/technology/early-facebook-google-employees-fight-tech.html.

BOWLES, NELLIE. "Me and My Numb Thumb: A Tale of Tech, Texts and Tendons." *The New York Times*, 19 May 2018, www.nytimes.com/2018/05/19/technology/smartphone-overuse-numb-thumb.html.

BRODY, JANE E. "Hooked on Our Smartphones." *The New York Times*, 9 Jan. 2017, www.nytimes.com/2017/01/09/well/live/hooked-on-our-smartphones.html.

BROMWICH, JONAH ENGEL. "Addicted to Your Smartphone? The Company That Made It Would Like You to Think So." *The New York Times*, 30

July 2015, www.nytimes.com/2015/07/31/technology/addicted-to-your-smartphone-the-company-that-made-it-would-like-you-to-think-so.html.

BROOKS, DAVID. "How Evil Is Tech?" *The New York Times*, 21 Nov. 2017, www.nytimes.com/2017/11/20/opinion/how-evil-is-tech.html.

BURROUGH, BRYAN. "When You Text Till You Drop." *The New York Times*, 12 May 2012, www.nytimes.com/2012/05/13/business/in-idisorder-a-look-at-mobile-device-addiction-review.html.

CARTER, C.D. "When Fantasy Football Becomes an Addiction." *The New York Times*, 27 Nov. 2012, fifthdown.blogs.nytimes.com/2012/11/27/when-fantasy-football-becomes-an-addiction/?searchResultPosition=17.

DAMOUR, LISA. "Parenting the Fortnite Addict." *The New York Times*, 30 Apr. 2018, www.nytimes.com/2018/04/30/well/family/parenting-the-fortnite-addict.html.

DOUGHERTY, CONOR. "Addicted to Your Phone? There's Help for That." *The New York Times*, 11 July 2015, www.nytimes.com/2015/07/12/sunday-review/addicted-to-your-phone-theres-help-for-that.html.

DREIFUS, CLAUDIA. "Why We Can't Look Away From Our Screens." *The New York Times*, 6 Mar. 2017, www.nytimes.com/2017/03/06/science/technology-addiction-irresistible-by-adam-alter.html.

FACKLER, MARTIN. "In Korea, a Boot Camp Cure for Web Obsession." *The New York Times*, 18 Nov. 2007, www.nytimes.com/2007/11/18/technology/18rehab.html.

FERGUSON, CHRISTOPHER J., AND PATRICK MARKEY. "Video Games Aren't Addictive." *The New York Times*, 1 Apr. 2017, www.nytimes.com/2017/04/01/opinion/sunday/video-games-arent-addictive.html.

FRIEDMAN, RICHARD A. "The Big Myth About Teenage Anxiety." *The New York Times*, 7 Sept. 2018, www.nytimes.com/2018/09/07/opinion/sunday/teenager-anxiety-phones-social-media.html.

GELLES, DAVID. "Tech Backlash Grows as Investors Press Apple to Act on Children's Use." *The New York Times*, 9 Jan. 2018, www.nytimes.com/2018/01/08/technology/apple-tech-children-jana-calstrs.html.

HAMILL, SEAN D. "Students Sue Prosecutor in Cellphone Photos Case." *The New York Times*, 26 Mar. 2009, www.nytimes.com/2009/03/26/us/26sextext.html.

HEFFERNAN, VIRGINIA. "Miss G.: A Case of Internet Addiction." *The New York Times*, 9 Apr. 2011, opinionator.blogs.nytimes.com/2011/04/09/miss-g-a-case-of-internet-addiction/.

ISAAC, MIKE. "Facebook Unveils Redesign as It Tries to Move Past Privacy Scandals." *The New York Times*, 30 Apr. 2019, www.nytimes.com/2019/04/30/technology/facebook-private-communication-groups.html.

IVES, MIKE. "Electroshock Therapy for Internet Addicts? China Vows to End It." *The New York Times*, 13 Jan. 2017, www.nytimes.com/2017/01/13/world/asia/china-internet-addiction-electroshock-therapy.html.

JOHNSON, DIRK. "Computers: An Extra Becomes an Essential." *The New York Times*, 18 June 1986, www.nytimes.com/1986/06/18/nyregion/computers-an-extra-becomes-an-essential.html.

KAMENETZ, ANYA. "Your Kid's Phone Is Not Like a Cigarette." *The New York Times*, 3 Mar. 2018, www.nytimes.com/2018/03/03/opinion/sunday/kids-technology-addiction-screentime.html.

KERSHAW, SARAH. "Hooked on the Web: Help Is on the Way." *The New York Times*, 1 Dec. 2005, www.nytimes.com/2005/12/01/fashion/thursdaystyles/hooked-on-the-web-help-is-on-the-way.html.

KLASS, PERRI, M.D. "Seeing Social Media More as Portal Than as Pitfall." *The New York Times*, 9 Jan. 2012, https://www.nytimes.com/2012/01/10/health/views/seeing-social-media-as-adolescent-portal-more-than-pitfall.html.

LEIVE, CINDI. "Sext and the Single Girl." *The New York Times*, 23 Mar. 2016, www.nytimes.com/2016/03/27/books/review/sext-and-the-single-girl.html.

LEWIS, PETER H. "When Machines Spawn Obsession." *The New York Times*, 13 Nov. 1988, www.nytimes.com/1988/11/13/business/the-executive-computer-when-machines-spawn-obsession.html.

LINDSTROM, MARTIN. "You Love Your IPhone. Literally." *The New York Times*, 1 Oct. 2011, www.nytimes.com/2011/10/01/opinion/you-love-your-iphone-literally.html.

MANJOO, FARHAD. "Even the Tech Elite Are Worrying About Tech Addiction." *The New York Times*, 9 Feb. 2018, www.nytimes.com/interactive/2018/02/09/technology/the-rise-of-a-visual-internet.html.

MANJOO, FARHAD. "You Don't Have to Feel Very Guilty About Using Your Smartphone While Parenting." *The New York Times*, 8 July 2014, bits.blogs.nytimes.com/2014/07/08/you-dont-have-to-feel-very-guilty-about-using-your-smartphone-while-parenting/.

MARRIOTT, MICHEL. "When Love Turns to Obsession, Games Are No Game." *The New York Times*, 12 Mar. 1998, www.nytimes.com/1998/03/12/technology/when-love-turns-to-obsession-games-are-no-game.html.

MILLER, CLAIRE CAIN. "How Social Media Gives Women a Voice." *The New York Times*, 9 Feb. 2018, www.nytimes.com/interactive/2018/02/09/technology/social-media-gives-women-a-voice.html.

MINSBERG, TALYA. "Read This. Then Put Away Your Phone." *The New York Times*, 2 Mar. 2019, www.nytimes.com/2019/03/01/business/addictive-technology.html.

THE NEW YORK TIMES. "The Government and the Web." *The New York Times*, 25 Aug. 2009, www.nytimes.com/2009/08/25/opinion/25tue3.html.

THE NEW YORK TIMES. "What They're Saying About Sexting." *The New York Times*, 27 Mar. 2011, www.nytimes.com/2011/03/27/us/27sextingqanda.html.

PARKER-POPE, TARA. "An Ugly Toll of Technology: Impatience and Forgetfulness." *The New York Times*, 7 June 2010, www.nytimes.com/2010/06/07/technology/07brainside.html.

RICHTEL, MATT. "Attached to Technology and Paying a Price." *The New York Times*, 7 June 2010, www.nytimes.com/2010/06/07/technology/07brain.html.

RICHTEL, MATT. "Growing Up Digital, Wired for Distraction." *The New York Times*, 21 Nov. 2010, www.nytimes.com/2010/11/21/technology/21brain.html.

RICHTEL, MATT. "The Lure of Data: Is It Addictive?" *The New York Times*, 6 July 2003, www.nytimes.com/2003/07/06/business/the-lure-of-data-is-it-addictive.html.

RICHTEL, MATT. "Phone Makers Could Cut Off Drivers. So Why Don't They?" *The New York Times*, 24 Sept. 2016, www.nytimes.com/2016/09/25/technology/phone-makers-could-cut-off-drivers-so-why-dont-they.html.

WAKABAYASHI, DAISUKE, AND BRIAN X. CHEN. "Google Says It Has Found Religion on Privacy." *The New York Times*, 7 May 2019, www.nytimes.com/2019/05/07/technology/google-privacy-tools.html.

WORTHAM, JENNA. "Feel Like a Wallflower? Maybe It's Your Facebook Wall." *The New York Times*, The New York Times, 9 Apr. 2011, www.nytimes.com/2011/04/10/business/10ping.html.

Index

This book is current up until the time of printing. For the most up-to-date reporting, visit www.nytimes.com.